THE GIRLS OF CANBY HALL

SOMETHING OLD, SOMETHING NEW

EMILY CHASE

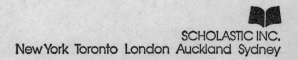

SCHOLASTIC INC.

New York Toronto London Auckland Sydney

ISBN 0-590-40391-5

12 11 10 9 8 7 6 5 4 3 2 1   6 7 8 9/8 0 1/9

Printed in the U.S.A.   01

First Scholastic printing, December 1986

Super Edition

THE GIRLS OF CANBY HALL

SOMETHING OLD, SOMETHING NEW

Super Edition

THE GIRLS OF CANBY HALL

CHAPTER ONE

Canby Hall School for Girls was snugly nestled in a small valley in a hilly part of Massachusetts, near the town of Greenleaf. Autumns there were mild and mostly sunny. This afternoon, though — the last Wednesday in October — the skies suddenly turned blue-gray and the winds slid down the hillsides and cut across the campus. Girls walking back to their dorms after classes were caught unprepared in light sweaters and jackets.

Among them, walking together along one of the many paths that crisscrossed the pretty campus, were Jane Barrett, October Houston, and Andrea Cord — sophomores, best friends, and roommates in Room 407, Baker House. The three of them found themselves huddling together as they walked, bending into the sharp wind.

"Argh," October said, slinging her knapsack full of books over one shoulder and wrap-

1

ping her arms around herself. She had set out this morning wearing only jeans and a flannel shirt. "Here comes my first real winter." Toby had just transferred to Canby Hall this year from Texas. She had never even seen snow firsthand.

"Well, coming from the Windy City," Andrea said, "a New England winter should seem mild to me." By "Windy City," she meant her hometown, Chicago, where winters were hard and long and blustery. Accustomed to the sudden changes in weather there, Andy was better prepared for the day than the other two. After listening to the weather report that morning, she'd thrown her khaki parachute vest on over her green turtleneck.

"Actually," said Jane Barrett, who came from nearby Boston, "I always look forward to winter. It's so pretty around here. Like those old Currier and Ives prints. But they can also be hazardous to your sanity once the snowball fights start. In winter, Canby Hall is major-league snowball-fight territory. The teachers stay in their houses mornings after big snowfalls. Even the guys from Oakley Prep are conspicuously absent. They're not dumb."

Jane was the only one of the three who had been at Canby Hall the previous year, and sometimes she liked to show off her Canby Hall savvy a little. The other two let her. The three of them indulged each other in lots of little ways. They had learned in their first-weeks together that they were radically different — Jane coming from Boston high society; Toby, a loner who'd lived all her life on a Texas ranch; and Andy, a Chicago black girl. The only way they could all live together and be friends was to cut each other a *lot* of slack.

By now they had reached the park at the center of the campus. Brightly colored leaves swirled down from the trees surrounding them. They came to the wishing pool, a Canby Hall landmark. Toby pulled a penny out of the watch pocket of her jeans, and threw it in with her eyes tightly closed.

When she opened them again, she ran a hand through her red curly hair and grinned sheepishly. She suspected the other two knew her wish: that Randy Crowell, who worked on his family's horse farm nearby, would decide that he was not too old to be interested in a fifteen-year-old girl — in particular a red-headed fifteen-year-old girl from Texas. So far, Randy, who was twenty, had held the line at friendship, but Toby was hoping for something more. She was patient, though. She figured she had waited fifteen years before running into a guy who'd caught her interest, so she could wait a while longer to see if *he* might get interested in her. In the meantime, she tried to help her case along with penny wishes.

The three roommates watched this particular penny sink through the leaf-covered, coppery green water and settle on the mossy bottom of the pool, amid hundreds of pennies from hundreds of wishes of Canby Hall girls. Most of these wishes had to do with boys, except during the week of final exams when a lot of them also had to do with geometry.

"Good afternoon, girls," said someone cutting into their reverie with a brisk, all-business voice. All three of them turned sharply, a little startled. The voice belonged to Patrice Allardyce, headmistress of Canby Hall, whose looks and personality were refrigerated — just a little warmer than freezing.

"I'm happy to see," she went on, "that you are stocking the pond, as it were. I'm sure you know that all the pennies are collected once a year, at Christmas, and turned into a check given to the Audubon Society, in honor of the many birds that bathe in this pond. It's been a tradition since the school opened in 1897."

Andy groaned silently. Another tradition. Although she liked the fact that Canby Hall was so deep in tradition, there were times when it got to be a little too much for her. She and Toby had started a kind of running joke about it.

Toby would roll out of bed and Andy would say, across the room, in a solemn tone, "Getting up in the morning — a tradition among Canby Hall girls since 1897."

Rushing, on their way out of the room,

Toby would stop Andy with a raised hand and say, "Being late for class — a tradition at Canby Hall for nearly a century."

But Ms. Allardyce was not in on this joke. She wouldn't think it was funny. Patrice Allardyce — or P.A., as almost everyone called her behind her back — *was* Canby Hall. She knew not only every tradition, but every rule — and enforced them rigorously. Girls who were out past dorm closing, or dressed sloppily for class, or were seen doing anything even resembling kissing a boy from Oakley Prep or Greenleaf High, were immediately called on the carpet. And Ms. Allardyce's carpet was not a pleasant place to be.

"Uh, oh, yes, Ms. Allardyce," Jane jumped in. "We were just having a moment of silence, thinking about all the wonderful birds that flock to Canby Hall. But now, alas, so many of them are flying away for the winter."

"Yes," Patrice Allardyce said, looking skyward. "There are things about autumn that are so sad." She paused, then went on with a new lilt in her voice. "But then there are other things that make the season so festive. So many wonderful fall traditions. Like this Saturday's All-Campus Leaf Rake. I assume you three have signed up."

"We were just heading for the sign-up sheet," Toby said, feeling sharp, simultaneous elbows in her ribs from either side for having just volunteered the three of them. Participating in the Leaf Rake meant getting up on Saturday morning at seven and spending two hours raking and singing along with what few other girls Ms. Allardyce had been able to pressure into signing up. The Leaf Rake was one of the school's *least* popular traditions.

"Good, good," Patrice Allardyce said, smiling with approval. Then she cinched the belt of her camel hair jacket tighter and set off toward the headmistress' house, leaving them with a small, fluttery wave good-bye.

"Leaf Rake," Andy said sarcastically to Toby, grabbing her, gangsterlike, by the collar of her shirt.

"*Seven* A.M.," Jane added, grabbing the other side of the collar, then teased, "We'll think of some way to get back at you for this. Sometime when you're least expecting it."

"Come on, you guys," Toby pleaded. "Give me a break. It won't be so bad. And it'll help Alison get off the hook. She told me she's only got two volunteers from Baker so far." Toby was referring to Alison Cavanaugh, their housemother, who was more like a good friend than a figure of authority to the girls in Baker House.

"Oh, I don't think Alison's all that concerned with Leaf Rakes lately," Andy said mysteriously.

"What do you mean?" asked Jane, tugging Andy's sleeve to nudge her into talking. Andy loved to "dish" — her term for gossiping.

Part of the dishing game was being coy about what you knew, making the other person drag it out of you. And so she answered in a round-about way.

"Well, am I the only one who's noticed how many Sundays Alison has been taking little train trips to Boston?"

"Maybe she has friends there," Toby said.

"Maybe," Andy said, and then didn't say anything more. This was another part of the game. So was changing the subject completely, which was what she did now. "You know, I did just horribly on my biology quiz. We were supposed to identify thirty crayfish parts. I only knew the outside ones like head and legs because I never could bring myself to do the stupid dissecting. I just went over to the infirmary that morning and told Nurse Zinger I had an awful stomachache. And then, when second period was over and the dissection was a thing of the past, my stomach suddenly got better."

"Neat trick," Toby said.

"Not so neat," Andy admitted. "The medicine The Zing gives out for stomachaches can't be much less disgusting than dissecting a crayfish."

"Enough about crayfish!" said Jane, who never had enough patience to really play the gossip game. "What about Alison's mystery visits to Boston?"

"Well," Andy said calmly, "I don't really

know what she's been up to. All I'm saying is that if *I* only had one day a week off, and *I* had a boyfriend as cute as Michael Frank right here on campus, I don't think I'd be off early every Sunday morning on the first train to Boston, and not be coming back until the last train on Sunday night."

"Another guy!" Jane whispered, pushing her long blond hair away from her face.

"That's how it looks to me," Andy said, "and if I do say so myself, I've got a pretty good nose for romance. Sometimes I think I'd make an incredible detective. For a couple of weeks now, I've been collecting clues on Alison."

"Like?" Toby prompted, narrowing her green eyes. She wasn't even sure what a romantic clue would be. Back home she rode her horse Max, and helped her dad out with chores around the ranch, and rode a battered old yellow bus every weekday to the consolidated county school. That was it. She hadn't even thought about boys until she'd met Randy last month. And her thoughts about him were so jumbled — more like raw, unprocessed feelings than real thoughts. Given this new state of confusion, she was very curious about romance, interested in any new bit of information on the subject. She wondered how Andy could tell Alison had a new romantic interest.

"Wellll," Andy said, "besides the weekly pilgrimages to Beantown, she's been walking around with *The Look* all over her face lately."

"The Look?" Toby said.

"Oh, you know, sort of a combination of glowing cheeks and zombie eyes. Like she's tuned into some fuzzy faraway radio station that's playing her favorite song. Plus, I've seen her twice in the past couple of weeks coming out of Cathy's Card Corner in Greenleaf." She looked at Toby and Jane, brushed her hands against each other and said, "I rest my case."

By the time the three of them got back to Baker House, they were thoroughly chilled. They ran up the wide stone steps and hurried to pull open the heavy oak doors. Inside, they were greeted with the hissing heat of the clanky old radiator in the entrance hall.

They went straight through to the mailroom. Andy had a package, as usual. Her family was lonesome for Andy in the way most Canby Hall girls were lonesome for home. They sent her about three goodie boxes a week. This was a small one. She held it up and shook it next to her ear, then grinned.

"Chocolate chip cookies," she said.

Jane had a letter from her sister Charlotte, a sophomore at Smith College. There was nothing for Toby. She wasn't expecting anything, anyway. Her father was as sparing with written words as he was with spoken ones, and she'd just gotten a letter from him last week.

"We might as well sign up for the Leaf Rake, as long as we're down here," Andy said. She nodded toward the announcement board, while at the same time bopping Toby on the head with the box of cookies for getting them all into this.

"Hey, will you look at this?" said Jane, who was already standing in front of the board with its dozens of push-pinned slips of paper. Announcements of yoga classes and rock bands forming, Spanish Club meetings. Ads for goldfish for sale and Friday rides to Boston. Messages from Baker girls to each other. *Brenda — Meet me at Pizza Pete's at five. Carrie.*

In the middle of this jumble was a neatly pinned sign-up sheet for the Leaf Rake, with a pencil hanging from a string pinned next to it — the perfect, efficient Patrice Allardyce touch. But that wasn't what Jane was staring at. Next to it was a large, scrawled marker notice reading: ALL-HOUSE ASSEMBLY TONIGHT AT SEVEN-THIRTY. IN THE LOUNGE. I HAVE AN IMPORTANT ANNOUNCEMENT AND WOULD LIKE EVERYONE THERE. ALISON. Jane turned to Andy. "What do you make of this?"

Andy just raised her eyebrows knowingly.

"Oh, come on," Jane said. "You don't really

think this can have anything to do with this *supposed* romance, this Fig Newton of your imagination, do you?"

"Can't it?" Andy said, casually inspecting her nails, which she'd done the night before in a dramatic new shade of burgundy. "We'll see."

CHAPTER TWO

Toby, Andy, and Jane had just set down their cafeteria trays on one of the big round wood tables in the dining hall. Toby turned and signaled to Maggie Morrison and Dee Adams, who were just coming out of the food line. Maggie and Dee lived next door to the three roommates, in 409 Baker, and were their closest friends. The five of them had dinner together most nights in the all-campus dining hall — referred to by most of the girls as "Hell's Kitchen."

Toby sat down and stared at what was on her plate.

"Did anyone look on the board and see what this is supposed to be?" she asked the table at large.

"Polynesian Delight," Maggie said, nodding her headful of wild brown curls knowingly.

"That means there's pineapple in it," Andy said.

"Right you are," Jane said, poking though hers, coming up with a yellow hunk speared on her fork. "How'd you know?"

"It's a code," Andy said. "All the casserole dishes here start with the same Generic Glop. They ship it in at night, in giant unmarked drums. And then they add different stuff to it. If they add spaghetti, it's Italian Delight. If they throw in some chili powder, it's Mexican Surprise."

"What about these desserts, then?" Dee asked.

Maggie jumped in here.

"My sister Dana had a theory about the desserts here. She figured that Patrice Allardyce had volunteered Canby Hall as an experimental test group for Foods of the Future. The desserts are molecularly restructured substances. They take something inedible, like a radial tire, and run it through a centrifuge and a blender and a few other scientific gizmos, and then they freeze-dry it. What comes out is a nice rubbery gunk. They use some of it for landfill, some for floor tile, and the rest for desserts at Canby Hall."

Everyone at the table laughed. They'd found that laughing was their best defense against the food at Canby Hall.

"So what does everybody think Alison's big announcement is going to be?" Dee asked, ripping open a foil packet of dressing and drizzling it over her salad. Dee nearly always opted for the salad bar over the cafeteria line, either because she was from California and into raw vegetables, or because from working in the cafeteria, she knew something the others didn't. Whatever she was eating, it had resulted in a tall, lean body, still tan from the California sun that had streaked her blond hair.

"Not sure," Jane said. "Something big, though. I think maybe she's got a new job somewhere else. Andy thinks it's about romance."

"Me, too," Maggie said. "I think she and Michael are announcing their engagement." Michael Frank was Canby Hall's guidance counselor, a favorite with the girls, and Alison's steady boyfriend for the past year or so.

"No," Andy said. "I think it's someone new. She's been going to Boston an awful lot lately. And she's going around all the time with this Cloud Nine grin. Meanwhile Michael has been looking like he needs to book a session with himself. Very depressed. Heartbreak, for sure."

"Andy!" Dee yelled, then laughed. "What have you been doing . . . reading Alison's diary?"

"Just paying attention," Andy said. "I don't miss much when it comes to my specialty . . . romance."

"So I hear," Maggie said.

"Just *what* do you hear, girl?" Andy asked, her brown eyes opening wide with interest.

"Oh, just that you've been seen around and about with a goony look on your face and Matt Hall's arm draped over your shoulder. That's all." Maggie was pretty good at "dishing" herself.

"Who's Matt Hall?" Toby asked. "And why am I always dead last to know?"

"There's nothing to know," Andy said.

"Matt Hall. Hmmm." Jane pondered. "Isn't he that sensitive-looking guy who did the lights for your dance recital?"

"Let's just hush up on this, all right?" Andy said, clearly embarrassed to be the object of this much scrutiny. She'd only been out for a couple of afternoon walks with Matt, and he hadn't called in nearly a week now, so maybe there was no romance to talk about. Although she talked a good game, Andy's real-life experience amounted to "going steady" with a boy who lived next door to her family. This had been in eighth grade and had lasted two weeks. In ninth grade, she'd had two dates to Friday night dances with a guy in her class, and his mother had driven them both times. Then she sat in the car while her son kissed Andy good-night at the door. Andy had thought she would die. She was about to die right now if somebody didn't change the subject, and that somebody was probably going to have to be her. She fished around in her brain for a great conversational gambit, but all she could come up with was, "Uh, hey, you guys, going to the Leaf Rake on Saturday? Room 407's all signed up!"

The others looked at each other and burst out laughing.

By five to seven, Andy and Jane and Toby, Dee and Maggie, and every other girl in Baker House were already down in the lounge. No one wanted to miss this announcement. Around Canby Hall, no one really knew where all the rumors came from, or who started them. They just raced through the air like a current. The rumor going around tonight was that Alison's announcement was going to be *juicy*.

She didn't show up until ten past seven, which was typical. Alison was a person in a perpetual dither. Looking for her glasses when they were already perched on top of her head. Losing the whole board of basement-storage locker keys. She was always setting the alarm on her watch to remind her to do something, and then when the alarm went off, she couldn't remember what it was time to do.

But in spite of this, or maybe because of it, the girls in Baker House loved Alison. She was a great cross between a girl and a grown-up. She could be counted on for good advice. She was incredibly supportive when you needed her. She would even get up in the middle of the night and make you cocoa if you'd had a terrible dream. And so she was like a great parent.

But in other ways she was very kidlike. She was big on practical jokes. She ate her Oreos by licking the frosting off first. And in spite of the no-pets rule at Canby Hall, she hid a cat named Doby up in her top-floor apartment.

Alison dressed like a latter-day hippie, in jeans and workshirts, and long flower-print skirts. Her hair was what Dee and Maggie called 'big hair,' a huge mass of curls tumbling around her shoulders.

Coming into the lounge, Alison looked more distracted than ever, all flushed and breathless. Her off-white, rough-weave cotton shirt was pulling loose from her beat-up khakis. She had put eyeliner on one eye, but not the other. She looked around nervously at all the girls sitting on the overstuffed chairs and sofas, and on the floor, and up in the cushioned window seats. She cleared her throat, then looked ready to start, but instead cleared her throat again. Finally she found her voice.

"First I want you all to know that I really love being your housemother. It's just that it looks like it's time for me to do something a little different."

"You're leaving us for another school, boo-hoo," someone shouted.

"Well, yes, actually, I will be leaving. But

not until the end of term. Before that, though, I'm going to be doing something else."

"You're getting married!" someone else shouted.

Alison looked startled, and then just nodded.

"You are?"

"Really?"

Everyone was prodding her for more, but it appeared she had grown momentarily too flustered to speak. And then somebody started up a chant.

"Mi-chael. Mi-chael. Mi-chael."

At this, Alison grew even more flustered and started waving to hush them. Finally she held up her hand in a "stop" sign.

"Please. Stop. It's . . . uh . . . well, it's not Michael."

At this, the whole room went silent and still. The only movement was Andy nudging Jane in the ribs as if to say, "Told you so."

"His name is David. David Gordon. He lives in Boston. I'll be moving there at Christmas, when the term is over. Maybe some of you have seen him on tv. He's the anchorman on the late news on Channel Six. Anyway, this has all been kind of sudden and I must admit I'm a little surprised myself, so I can understand if you are, too. But I hope you'll all be happy for me and come to the wedding. It'll be right here on campus in the chapel on the Saturday after Thanksgiving."

At this piece of information, somebody started humming "Here Comes the Bride," and all the girls rushed to Alison to give her hugs. A lot of them would have preferred she were marrying Michael, but she was clearly so happy that it was impossible not to be happy for her.

Jane and Toby and Andy and Maggie and Dee were among the last of Alison's well-wishers, and they wound up walking upstairs with her. They had a million questions, which she tried to answer.

Was David cute? (yes)

Where did she meet him? (at a party)

What kind of dress was she going to wear? (her great-grandmother's lace wedding gown)

Where would they live? (in his apartment in the Back Bay area of Boston)

At the door to the fourth-floor hallway, she left them to head up to The Penthouse, her top-floor apartment. "I guess before I do anything else I'd better call my maid of honor."

"Who's that going to be?" they all wanted to know.

She smiled, tapped Maggie's shoulder, and said, "Someone *you* know very well."

"My sister!" Maggie shouted. "Dana!"

Alison smiled and said, "I'm hoping Faith and Shelley will come, too."

"Oh, great!" Maggie said. "The new girls of 407 and the old girls of 407 . . . all here at once!"

Dana Morrison, Faith Thompson, and Shelley Hyde had shared 407 Baker for three years before graduating last June. Now they lived in very different places. Maggie smiled, thinking of how the wedding would bring the three old friends back to Canby Hall, if only for one brief weekend.

It was only noon in Hawaii. Dana was taking her five-mile run along the beach with the family dog, Harry. She was spending this year with her father and her stepmother, Eve, and their little baby, Joey. They lived in a beach house, which was great for Dana in lots of ways. She loved running along the ocean in the afternoons, then taking a swim in it later, then falling asleep to the crashing of the waves beyond her bedroom window.

Now, though, she heard something over the roar of the waves. She looked up. It was Eve, standing on the redwood deck of the house, waving to Dana. When Dana got closer, Eve shouted, "Phone!" and mimed putting a receiver to her ear.

"Long distance," she told Dana, as she held open the door for her to run past.

When Dana put the receiver to her ear, all she could hear at first was crackling static.

"Hello!" she shouted.

"Dana?" It sounded vaguely like Alison, a very tiny Alison a million miles away. "Can you hear me?"

"Sort of. But I think Alexander Bell might have had a better connection on his first call."

She could hear Alison laugh in the distance.

"Listen. I can't talk long. I don't even want to know the rate between Massachusetts and Maui. The thing is, I'm getting married! At Thanksgiving. I want you and Faith and Shelley to be here for it. And I want *you* to be my maid of honor."

"Oh, Alison! That's what I am — honored! Of course I'll try to get there. I have to ask my dad. I was planning to come home for Christmas, but I think I can talk him into letting me go at Thanksgiving instead. I really want to be part of this. I love you and Michael both so much."

"Oh. Well, the other thing is that it's not Michael."

"Wow. This connection is *really* terrible! I thought you said it's not Michael."

"Dana. I've fallen in love with someone new. His name's David Gordon. He's a newscaster on tv in Boston."

"Oh."

"Dana. Surely you can come up with a little more enthusiasm than that."

"I'm sure he's great," Dana said tersely, still thinking of poor Michael . . . dumped.

"David's better than great," Alison responded. "But you'll see for yourself when you get out here. Oh boy, I'd better get off. This is probably costing a small fortune. And

I've still got calls to Shelley and Faith to make."

"Oh, Alison, let me do that. Please. I love being the bearer of surprise news."

"You mean you want the chance to gossip about this with them," Alison said perceptively.

Dana — caught out — had to laugh.

"All right," Alison gave in. "You call them. But then it's also your responsibility to get them to come to the wedding. I really need you three here. I've never gotten married before. I'm pretty much in a state of nervous collapse already. I can't stand thinking I'm going to have to walk down that aisle with everyone turned, looking at me. And what if, at the last minute, David gets cold feet and doesn't show up?"

"That only happens in bad movies," Dana assured her. "Everything will go fine. And if you're a total basket case by then, Faith and Shelley and I will carry you down the aisle in a basket."

As soon as Dana hung up from the call with Alison, she dialed the area code for Rochester, New York, then the number of the boarding house where Faith had a room near the campus of the state university there. Some other girl answered and Dana hopped nervously from foot to foot, looking toward the kitchen where Eve was feeding the baby. She didn't want her to know she was making this call. She figured it would be easier to just deal with her dad about it when the bill came in.

Finally, after what seemed like about half an hour, but was probably only a couple of minutes, Faith's voice came on the other end of the line.

"Faith?"

"Dana?! I can't believe it. Where are you?"

"Hawaii."

"Wow. What's up? Must be something big if you're calling from all the way out there . . . and it's the middle of the day where you are, isn't it?"

"Yeah, it's a hot sunny afternoon and the surf's up."

"Wretch. It's night and cold and the rain's coming down in buckets here. But come on, tell me what's going on?"

"Alison's getting married, and before you say you're so happy for her and Michael, you should know it's *not* Michael."

"Oh, my."

"Exactly."

"Well, if she threw over Michael, who has got to be one of the most terrific guys in the world, it must be for some guy who's incredibly rich and famous and good-looking. Robert Redford's already married, so who does that leave?"

"David Gordon. Boston newscaster."

"You know," Faith mused. "I think I remember seeing him on tv. Blond. Cute in a craggy sort of way. Real deep voice."

"I'm going to be maid of honor. She wants me and you and Shelley to come out for it."

"Oh, I'll come. I wouldn't want to miss this for the world. Have you called Shelley yet?"

"No, I was just about to."

"Let me instead. I don't want your father killing you when he sees the phone bill. Besides, I want to see if they've got phones out there in Iowa yet."

Dana laughed, but cautioned Faith, "Don't let *her* hear you say that. You know how she hates jokes about how small town she is."

Shelley was memorizing her role in a science fiction play as Ufra, Princess of the Galaxies of Tepan. She was in her dorm room at the University of Iowa, pacing back and forth with her script. She picked up the receiver and, still absorbed in the play, shouted into it.

"You must flee the galaxies at once, Morbu. Now that the Mind Controllers have the secret of telesynthesis, you are in grave danger."

"Huh?" Faith said. "I must have the wrong number, or wrong planet, or something."

"Faith?" Shelley said.

"I think so," Faith teased. "Or maybe I'm really Morbu, but just don't realize it."

Shelley laughed. "Oh, Faith, I'm trying to memorize this part. The thing is, I can't make

heads or tails of science fiction. Most of the
time I can't even remember what galaxy we're
warring with, or if Morbu's my father or my
brother. And in rehearsal, my ray gun's always
going on the blink. But that's not what you
called to find out."

"Actually it was. I was going to ask how
your ray gun was, then I was going to mention
that Alison's getting married at Thanksgiving,
and wants us to come to the wedding."

"Oh, of course I'll come. She and Michael
are the two people in the world I'd most like
to see married."

"Not so fast," Faith said. "Scratch Michael,
pencil in David Gordon."

"David Gordon? Who's that, and why is he
even daring to think he can marry Alison?"

"I'm not sure exactly what's going on. We'll
know more when we get there. Maybe we'll
be crazy about this new guy."

"Maybe," Shelley said, sounding uncertain.
"But what if we're not?"

Faith laughed, then said, "Well, you could
always bring your ray gun."

Later that night, back at Canby Hall, Toby,
Jane, and Andy were all scrunched together
on Jane's bed, peering at the screen of her
five-inch mini-tv, watching the late news on
Channel Six.

"Today, a new proposal for balancing the
federal budget," the anchorman was saying.

They watched and listened in silence until the commercial break.

"I think he's cute," Andy said.

"Too much hair," Jane said. "And it's too in place. Like it was sprayed. And that tan. Give me a break. Who has a tan in Boston in late October? He probably goes to one of those booths."

"What's your vote, Toby?" Andy asked.

"I'm not sure yet. I think I'd have to see him out in the open, out from behind that stupid desk. It helps me get an idea about people to see them move around. It's the same with horses."

When the other two started laughing, Toby didn't understand why.

"You two just don't understand. Horses and people are a lot alike."

"Maybe you're right," Jane said in her teasing tone. "I think when David comes here to see Alison, you ought to check his teeth."

"*And* his hooves," Andy added.

"Oh, of course his hooves," Jane said. "I wouldn't marry anyone without making sure his hooves were in good shape."

"You *guys*." Toby pleaded for them to stop. The other two could tell something was bothering her, and that it wasn't their teasing.

"Come on," Jane said. "Out with it. No secret brooding allowed in here."

"Well," Toby said, putting her thumb in her mouth, then quickly pulling it out — a flashback to childhood that happened when she was upset, "what I'm wondering is what I'm supposed to wear to this wedding. Somehow I don't think velvet bows on my boots will do, and I don't have any idea where to even begin to put together a really dressy get-up! The only dress I have is the one I wore to the Oakley Prep dance. And even I know that's not right for a wedding!"

"Well," Andy said, "isn't it lucky that you just happen to be rooming with two of Canby Hall's fashion pacesetters? We'll take you out to the mall on Saturday and get going on this!"

"Project D.U.T.," Jane said. When the other two flashed her question mark looks, she said, "Dress Up Toby."

CHAPTER THREE

When Andy's alarm went off at six on Saturday morning, all three roommates sat up startled, like jack-in-the-boxes.

"What time is it?" Toby asked through a huge yawn.

"Six," Andy said.

"What *day* is it?" said Jane in a muffled voice. She had burrowed back under the covers and put her pillow over her head.

"Saturday," Andy said.

"Saturday?!" both Jane and Toby yelled.

"It's the *Leaf Rake*," Andy said in a tone of total disgust. "We've got to get up."

The room went up in groans.

"Tell them I got sick," Toby said.

"Tell them I died," Jane said.

"Come on, you two. We promised. And you know there isn't going to be a huge crowd. If we don't show up, we're sure to be missed . . . by P.A. She'll mark us down in her little red demerit book under 'Lacking in School Spirit,' and give us the fish eye for the rest of our days here. You know how they say she's like an elephant."

"You mean big and gray with a tough hide?" Toby teased.

"You *know* what I mean," Andy said. "She never forgets."

"Okay, okay, I'll get up. Just give me my rake and basket," Jane said, blearily bounding out of bed in a flurry of mock spiritedness. She grabbed a couple of knit caps off the hat hooks and started shaking them like pom-poms. "Let me at those leaves. Onward to a leafless Canby Hall!"

The other two caught her goofiness and joined in, making up a cheer as they went along.

> *Rake 'em back.*
> *Rake 'em back.*
> *Waaaay back!*

"Pyramid!" Jane shouted, and the other two groaned and dropped down on all fours, letting her climb onto their backs and shake the hats with a final shout of, "Yeah, Canby Hall!"

At this point, Maggie Morrison, blinking sleepily behind the lenses of her glasses, peered through the doorway and said, "I hope this is just a bad dream I'm having."

The pyramid collapsed into a heap on the

floor and Jane said, "Oh, it is, Maggie. We're just a mirage. Go back to sleep and we'll disappear."

Maggie nodded and shuffled out the door, first going down the hall the wrong way, then passing the doorway again a few seconds later, this time heading in the direction of her room.

Toby, Jane, and Andy started laughing the muffled, unstoppable laughter that always seemed to happen to them precisely when they knew they should *not* be laughing.

They were still falling into periodic bouts of laughter when they got down to the Leaf Rake. There was a grand total of seven girls out on the front lawn of Baker, including themselves. Alison was also there, looking happier than anyone possibly could in this situation, unless she were totally in love.

Patrice Allardyce was heading up the leaf rakers, wearing an outfit she undoubtedly thought of as "woodsy." Jane had noticed that although Ms. Allardyce was ultrafashionable when it came to dressing up, when the occasion was casual, she was completely lost, and wound up wearing something that looked like a disguise. Like this morning. She was raking away vigorously in red plaid pants, a gold wool jacket, and a brimmed felt hat with a little brush stuck in the band at the side.

"Oh, good!" she said enthusiastically when Toby, Jane, and Andy arrived. "Reinforcements! Now we have enough to start singing.

I thought we could all do some rounds. You know, we could start with 'Row, Row, Row Your Boat' and work our way up to some more complex ones."

"Oh, Patrice," Alison said, breaking out of her fog to come to the girls' rescue, "I think it still might be a little early for singing. Why don't we all just work awhile in silent communion with nature?"

Patrice Allardyce loved nature, especially the nature around Canby Hall, and so agreed to this plan. Which left the three roommates free to just grab rakes and big plastic garbage bags and start to work. The first half hour was hard. None of them were really awake, and there was a damp morning chill in the air. But then the strong fall sun started blanketing them with warmth, and then Alison came around with a big thermos dispenser of hot cider. Cider was one of the great autumn treats around Canby Hall, as it was pressed from apples grown in the orchard out by the skating pond. Each of the girls had three cups, as well as two of the ham and cheese croissants Alison had gotten earlier from the new French bakery in Greenleaf.

"Hey," Toby said, "this is beginning to seem like not such a bad idea."

The other two nodded with mouths full of croissant. And when they went back to work, it was with renewed spirit. By nine-thirty, they had cleared off the lawns of all three dorms —

Addison, Baker, and Charles — and actually felt a little proud of themselves. Toby was the happiest. Back home on the ranch in Texas, every one of her Saturdays began like this, doing chores. She hadn't realized how much she'd been missing outdoor work.

"Maybe we could just keep going," she told the other two. "Do the whole darn campus!"

"You're kidding, of course," said Jane, who came from a wealthy Boston family. Any previous leaves in her life had been raked for her. This morning hadn't been as bad as she thought, but she was happy to be done with the job.

Just then, there was a loud sputtering roar from the direction of the road. A small, old, green sports car with the top down came into view, then pulled to a stop in front of the leaf-raking crew. The driver was blond and extremely handsome. He was wearing reflector aviator sunglasses, a bomber jacket, and a wool scarf that matched the car. When he pulled off the glasses, it was clear that the scarf and car also matched his eyes. Bottle green. It was David Gordon. All three roommates recognized him from seeing him on tv the night before. In person he was even better looking.

Although there were at least a couple of dozen girls there by now, he smiled a dazzling smile that was for one person only. Alison. She caught it like a fielder catching a ball, and tossed a large smile of her own back at him.

The girls just stood watching this scene, as if it were in some movie.

"You still going to check out those teeth?" Jane teased Toby under her breath. "They look pretty good to me."

Toby blushed a little, and waved Jane away.

"He kind of looks like a younger version of Paul Newman, doesn't he?" Andy said. "Only with green eyes instead of blue."

"He looks like he's got Alison under a spell," Toby observed. "Is that what love is like . . . true love?"

Jane thought about how she sometimes felt when she came downstairs and found her new boyfriend, Cary Slade, leaning against one of the pillars in the entrance hall of Baker, waiting for her.

She told Toby, seriously, "Well, if it's a spell, it's one that goes two ways. Look how Alison makes *him* smile. And how he makes her eyes light up. I don't ever remember seeing her looking like that at Michael."

"Speaking of whom . . ." said Andy, leaning against her rake, noticing the approach of Canby Hall's guidance counselor. He was coming from behind Addison and so saw only the leaf-raking party, which had grown through the morning to about thirty girls. Obscured from his view was David Gordon getting out of his sports car and loping across the lawn to swoop Alison up into his arms. Michael, unfortunately, got through the crowd just in time to get a close-up view — too close for comfort. For a moment, he stood there in a kind of stunned daze. Then abruptly, the daze turned into an angry glare. He turned on his heel without a word and stalked off toward faculty housing.

Alison was so caught up by David that she didn't even see this. Some of the girls did, though. Toby did. And in that moment she realized that these feelings she was having about Randy Crowell were just the beginning. At some point in her future she was probably going to wind up feeling as good as Alison and David, or as bad as Michael. For a brief moment, she wished she could just go back to being a kid where everything was safe and understandable. She felt a little like she was being parachuted into strange territory at night, with no compass, and no map.

"Earth to Toby," Andy was saying.

"Come on," Jane added. "We've been released by the warden." She nodded to indicate Patrice Allardyce. "Turn in your rake and let's hurry. We can change and catch the noon bus over to the mall and get started on finding this super-mega-ultra-outfit for Toby's grand entrance at the wedding."

"Yeah," Andy said, rumpling Toby's red curls. "We're going to make you look so ravishing, you'll have to be careful you don't upstage the bride!"

* * *

Sitting side-by-side on the long seat in the very back of the bus heading for the Greenleaf Corners Mall, Jane, Toby, and Andy were lounging lazily, their legs stretched out in front of them, talking about their lives at home. This was a favorite topic of theirs. They couldn't stop being amazed at what different worlds they had come from.

"Toby, just how big, or should I say small, is Rattlesnake Creek?" Andy asked.

"Oh, well, let me see. Thirty-eight. No. Old Mrs. Reese passed on over the summer. So, thirty-seven."

"Thirty-seven!?" the other two both said.

"Well, that is unless Florence Cudahy already had her baby. So it *could* be thirty-eight after all."

"Are there really any rattlesnakes around there?"

" 'Course there's rattlers."

"What do you do about them?" Jane asked.

"Try not to aggravate 'em," Toby said with a slow smile.

The mall was out on the edge of town, by the highway. It had several trendy clothes shops, and Jane figured they were bound to find something for Toby at one of them.

"Oooo," Andy said. "Let's go in here — New Waves."

"Too punk," Jane said, waving her hand at the store in dismissal as she led them past it.

"We don't want foil and fluorescent today. We're shopping for a wedding. I think we ought to look first at Sandra's Styles. They've got nice dress-up stuff." She tried to keep her tone upbeat. She could see that Toby was getting a little grim and reluctant as the actual shopping drew nearer. What Jane had in mind for her was an elegant tailored dress. But she knew that saying the word "dress" to Toby would be like waving a red cape in front of a mad bull. No, she'd have to work up to that.

Luckily, before they got to any clothes store, they passed The Cookie Jar. They had gone from the Leaf Rake to the bus without stopping for lunch, and so were incredibly hungry. Also, although the three of them were all into healthy eating, they all agreed that there were five basic food groups: grain, milk, vegetables, meat — and cookies! And so they got some chocolate chips for Jane, some peanut butters for Andy, some oatmeal-raisins for Toby, and took a break before taking on Project Dress-Up Toby. When they were finished, Toby leaped to her feet, and said, "All *right*!" — slapping their hands the way Andy had shown them the boys back in her high school did. "Let's go!"

The dressy clothes were in a front section of Sandra's Styles. Jane scanned the racks and muttered to Andy under her breath, "Let's start her off with pants outfits. I'm not sure she ever wore a dress back in Python Gulch."

Andy nodded and went down to the end of the rack. She started helping Toby out, finding out what colors she liked, what fabrics, what styles. Pretty soon Jane came back with a couple of outfits. One was a pair of pleated pants and a slouchy jacket in forest green, with a shirt in green and rust stripes. The other was an outfit coordinated with a beige wool skirt and a beige silk shirt with a white and gray striped gangster vest. Toby liked both of these and sailed straight into the fitting room with them.

Jane looked at Andy in mild amazement. "Wow. I thought we were going to have to drag her kicking and screaming into the fitting room. Maybe this is going to be easier than I thought."

Toby came out in the green outfit, which, although none of them could say exactly *why*, just wasn't her. The beige outfit, though, was much more on target and Toby wanted to buy it immediately.

"Not so fast," Jane said. "We're only beginning. We have to be wise consumers here. While you were in there, I found a couple more things." She handed Toby half a dozen hangers. This selection included more pants outfits, a suit with a skirt, and, at the very back, a dress.

Toby came out and modeled each one,

growing bolder with each outfit, clearly enjoying the attention she was getting from Andy
and Jane. She was gradually getting into the
spirit of fooling around with clothes, something she had never done before. By the time
she came out in the dress, she was thoroughly
into the costume-party atmosphere.

"Hey. Look at me in this! A dress, hmmm?
And not one my aunt in Dallas sent. Hey, are
there any more out there?"

"Of course," Jane said, laughing.

"Could you bring me some? Fancier than
this. I'm sort of getting a kick out of seeing
what I look like in all this stuff. Bring me
something that makes me look like I grew up
in New York City, instead of Rattlesnake
Creek."

And so Jane headed for the designer racks,
and brought back a blue dress with forties
shoulder pads and a splash of sequins across
the front. When Toby came out in it, she
didn't just walk out of the fitting room, she
emerged. Then twirled, then did a ballet-style
reach up onto her toes. Then, to the applause
of her roommates, she took a deep bow.

And came up to meet the amused stare of
Randy Crowell, who was standing, thumbs
hooked in the belt loops of his jeans, watching
this antic display through the store window
facing onto the mall.

Seeing him froze Toby in motion. Her jaw

dropped. Her heart sank. Her face blushed. Her arms broke out in goose bumps. She was totally and utterly mortified. She longed for a trap door to open beneath her and let her drop mercifully out of sight. But this didn't happen, and so the only way she could get out of this was to run back into the safety of the fitting room, where she slumped down in the corner and began to cry.

Until now, she knew she had impressed Randy as a sensible, mature, head-on-her-shoulders sort of girl. Which is exactly how she *wanted* to impress him. She didn't want him to think she was some silly, dingbatty, conceited thing, who twirled around in fancy dresses as if she thought she was some kind of celebrity. And yet this was precisely what he must think now.

She thought again of that little smile on his face. It must have been amusement at how foolish she looked. And thinking this made her sad turn sharply into mad. Why was she crying? What was the matter with her? Back in Texas she couldn't have cared less what anybody thought. And if some guy took to thinking he was better than her, well she'd just show him by riding faster or roping better than he. That generally wiped the smirk off his face.

But then she raised her head and looked across the fitting room in the mirror and saw herself, collapsed down in the corner like a dropped marionnette, rigged up in the stupid dress, and she began crying all over again.

At this point, Jane and Andy came in after her. Neither of them said anything. Andy sat down on the floor next to Toby and gave her a hug of reassurance. Jane took the beige outfit and went out to charge it. Toby could pay her back when she calmed down. And she'd have something to wear to the wedding. Something she liked.

When Jane got out to the counter, Randy was standing there, looking ill-at-ease now, rocking nervously back and forth on his heels.

"Did I upset her or something?" he asked in that dense way guys had that always made Jane both love them and want to kill them at the same time.

"Oh," she said, "it wasn't your fault. She was fooling around for us and didn't expect to see you. She thinks she looked dumb."

"Well, I can't go back there and tell her myself, so I'd appreciate it if you'd pass along the message that I thought she looked, well . . . real pretty." And then it was his turn to feel embarrassed. "I guess I'd better get out of here," he said, looking around nervously at the all-female preserve of Sandra's Styles.

Later, on the way out of the mall, when Jane passed along Randy's message to a calmed-down Toby, she blinked as if someone had just taken a flash picture of her.

"He said *that*?! Really? Hmmm." She thought about this for a moment, then said with a shy smile, "I *did* look pretty cute in that dress, didn't I?"

CHAPTER FOUR

Toby was only tongue-tied for the first minute or so when Randy called on Sunday morning. Then it was all right. He was just regular Randy and she was just regular Toby again, and the odd scene out at the mall the day before seemed far, far away.

"Beautiful fall day out there," he said. "Might be the last of the year. Better take advantage of my offer."

"What's that?" she asked.

"Free horse rides for redheads. Maxine needs a workout, and you're the only human in these parts brave or foolish enough to get on her." Maxine was a new horse the Crowells had just bought. Randy had named it after Max, Toby's own horse back in Texas.

"Oh, she's not that wild. Not if you sweet-talk her a little. Saddle her up and I'll be right over. I'll run all the way."

The Crowell horse farm was one of the largest in the state. Randy worked on it along with the rest of his family. It was more love than work, really. He loved horses, and loved the gentle Massachusetts countryside. Like Toby, he really enjoyed being outdoors, close to nature. It was one of the things they had in common. Mostly they didn't talk about this, but sometimes she'd tell him about how beautiful Texas was. Other times, Randy would recite to her poems about nature and wildlife and the seasons. At first she'd been surprised at this. She had never met a guy who spouted poetry. Actually, she'd never met *anyone* who spouted poetry. But then she started liking it. He never told her who'd written these poems, and so she was never sure if it was some famous poet, or himself.

Today he didn't have any poems. They just rode hard for a while, giving Maxine a good run. When they got to the big maple grove north of Greenleaf, they reined the horses to a walk and began talking. Toby brought up the previous day so she could explain it to him.

"That foolishness out at the mall was all about fixing me up to go to this wedding."

"Oh," he said. "Who's getting married? Patrice Allardyce?"

"Now, wouldn't that be something?" Toby asked. "But try to imagine someone classy enough for her to marry. Maybe some prince. Or a duke. It would have to be at least a duke. No, it's Alison who's getting married."

"To that shrink guy?"

"Michael? No, that's what everyone thought, but it turns out she's gone off and fallen like a ton of bricks for some tv anchorman from Boston. I think she decided to marry him in about ten minutes. I guess that happens to some people."

"Don't be so smug. It could happen to you."

"Me? I'm *never* getting married."

"That's what you say now," Randy said. "Lots of people say that at fifteen. I did. Then you get different ideas."

"You mean you want to get married?"

"Someday. Sure. Why not? You want me to be an old hermit all alone in my shack in the woods?" He hunched over in his saddle, impersonating this ancient recluse, and shook an invisible stick angrily at her.

Toby laughed and said, "Well, actually, you'd make a kind of cute old hermit. But if you want to get married, go ahead. You have my blessing. But not me. I don't want to wash out anybody's socks every night."

At this remark, Randy reined his horse to a stop and turned to look at Toby with question marks in his eyes.

"Well," Toby tried to explain, "that's what wives of cowboys do."

"Who says you have to marry a cowboy?"

"Well, that's pretty much all there is around Rattlesnake Creek."

"But you're not *in* Rattlesnake Creek anymore. Maybe you'll wind up staying out here. Not too many guys here expect to get their socks washed. My mom and dad take turns doing the laundry. They both work hard on the farm, so it's only fair. Me and my brothers all do our own."

"Is that right?" Toby said, scratching her head in amazement. "Well, if there were no sock washing in the bargain, I might do it. If only it didn't mean changing my name. When Bobby Bill Smerdley was after me, I realized that if I actually fell in love with him — which, if you knew Bobby Bill, you'd know was impossible, but say I did — well, I'd have to give up an extremely cool name like Houston, to become Toby Smerdley. Well, forget it."

"But lots of women don't change their names anymore when they get married."

"They don't?"

"Welcome to Massachusetts, *and* the twentieth century," Randy teased.

"Well, it sounds as though I might just like it here. Maybe I'll even reconsider the possibility of getting married. Not to you, though. I could never do that." Toby had found that, although she could say almost nothing to

Randy if it was serious, she could say the most outrageous stuff to him without even blinking, as long as it was teasing or fooling around.

"Why not?" he said, mock hurt in his voice.

"Well, I couldn't marry a man I could beat in a horse race, now could I?" she said, laughing as she dug her knees into Maxine's flanks and shouted, "Heeeeooowww!" to start her into a gallop.

Before Randy could blink in surprise, Toby already had a quarter-mile lead on him. She rode Maxine over the ridge, down through the valley, and brought her into the farmyard of the Crowell place at a brisk canter. Randy was close behind, but still couldn't catch up. Toby slid from the saddle, while Maxine was still trotting toward the fence. When Randy came around the barn, he saw Toby leaning against a fencepost, whistling and pretending to be leisurely inspecting her nails.

"All right. All right," he said, laughing. "So don't marry me. I wouldn't marry a girl who cheats on her starts, anyway. We Crowells have principles, you know." He slid off his horse and sat on the top rail of the fence she was leaning against. The afternoon sun was golden now, the trees alive with autumn colors, the sharp coolness of all air underlying it all. The two of them didn't say anything for a while. They had developed an easiness with each other. They could do this — just be together, without having to say anything. When someone finally spoke, it was Randy.

"So. Have you ever been to a wedding before?"

Toby shook her head and said, "Not really. Leastwise, not one like this. Back home, if two people want to get hitched, they usually have Judge Sanders or one of the traveling ministers do it, and then they have a party in the high school gym, or a square dance out in someone's barn. Everybody wears their cleanest jeans. In Rattlesnake Creek, *that's* dressing up. Alison's getting married in the chapel on campus. Very fancy. Then there's going to be a reception in the student center. I think it's going to be huge. All her friends and family, and his, plus all the girls in Baker. Plus she's having her old student friends come back for it. The three girls who used to live in our room. One of them — she's Maggie's sister — is going to be her maid of honor. Coming in all the way from Hawaii. Dina."

"Dana," Randy said, his voice lowered almost to a whisper.

"You know her?" Toby said.

He nodded slowly, and slid down off the fence rail until he was standing next to Toby, and then he said, "Remember I told you I used to go with a Canby Hall girl and it didn't work out?"

"It was *her*?"

"Yes."

"Do you still feel bad about it? I mean, would you want to see her when she comes in?"

"Oh, no! I think you'll find me . . . well . . . hard to find that weekend. Hawaii is about the right amount of distance between me and Dana Morrison. Canby Hall is a little close for comfort."

Suddenly and inexplicably, Toby felt a wave of jealousy rush through her. But why? All he was saying was that Maggie's sister had stung him a year or two ago. What could such a piece of ancient history have to do with her? And then she began to see the connection. She couldn't stand that he could feel so strongly about some girl a couple of years and thousands of miles away. Some girl who didn't even care enough about him to hang onto him. For this faraway Dana his eyes glazed over with longing. For Toby he had light affection, and teasing jokes, and buddy-buddy gestures like rumpling her curly hair. She bet he'd never rumpled Dana's hair. Dana probably didn't have rumpleable hair. She probably had long, silky hair, and a great smile, and one of those laughs that sounded like breaking glass and drove boys crazy. Suddenly, without even having met her, Toby felt a brief flash of wanting to *be* Dana Morrison.

She had to get away from Randy. She

couldn't take any more of watching him languish in these Dana blues. She gave him a little punch in the arm to let him know she was going. He nodded. Neither of them said good-bye. Toby just walked off along the fence of the corral, whistling and looking around her, trying unsuccessfully to bring back the good feelings she'd been having about this day.

While Toby and Randy were riding out under the peaceful blue New England skies, Jane was spending her Sunday in the dark, damp, noisy basement of Marsh Hall. Marsh was Cary Slade's dorm, and the basement activity room there was where he and the other guys in his band, Ambulance, practiced on Sundays.

Two months ago, if you'd asked Jane Barrett to spend a Sunday hanging out listening to a rock group practice, she would have looked at you as if you'd lost your mind. Back then she mostly loved classical music and opera. She liked some rock, but was very picky about her favorites.

In those days Jane had thought, for the most part, that music, like one's family money, ought to be at least a few generations old. She liked classical music in much the same way she liked antique quilts and traditional furniture. She thought things acquired value as they stood the test of time. Most rock music had seemed raw and crude to her.

And worse than the music were the musicians — a scruffy bunch with their tangled hair and leather pants. Give her a guy in chinos and a tweed jacket any day. A guy with a nice neat haircut and a family that *her* family knew. A guy like her longtime Boston boyfriend, Cornelius Worthington III. Neal.

Of course all these attitudes were pre-Cary Slade. And all of them had changed that fateful night early in the term when she'd gone over to a dance at Oakley Prep where Ambulance was playing. She hadn't even gone to enjoy herself, only to take notes for a writing assignment on "An Unusual Experience."

It was there she'd first seen Cary. She'd taken seven pages of notes on him. Everything about him was an unusual experience. His punked-out clothes. His earring. The way he wore sunglasses inside, at night. She stared at him so long and hard, trying to absorb every detail, as her writing teacher had advised, that he'd thought she was flirting with him. Imagine! The nerve. And then between sets, he'd come over and started talking to her. The most surprising thing about him was that he, too, came from the high-society circles in Boston. He and Jane had even gone to the same ballroom dance class in grammar school.

But since then, he'd rebelled against all that. He'd traded in his school blazer and rep tie for a guitar and a chip on his shoulder. Part of what he'd turned his back on were girls like Jane, and so as it turned out, he was more critical of her than she was of him.

"I already know all about you," he'd told her once. "You brush your hair a hundred strokes a night, even when you're really tired."

"Yes," she'd said, "and I floss, and I never forget to sign out of the dorm."

"And you like your parents," he'd said.

"Of course. They're my best friends."

"Argh," he'd said, pretending to strangle himself. "How can I be so crazy about you?"

"Because although I *am* all the ways you say I am, I am also uniquely myself and surprise you at quite a few turns. And besides, you're a fool for blondes."

"It's true," he'd sighed, and had given up the argument. At least for that day. But they'd had it again several times in these weeks they'd been seeing each other.

Today, Jane brought Andy along with her. Andy loved rock, and was also looking for an opportunity to "accidentally" run into Matt Hall, who did the lights for Ambulance's shows.

They got a couple of diet colas out of the soda machine in the basement hallway, then came into the activity room by the back door and found themselves a place to sit in a dark recess in the back, on an old folding table against the wall. The band was working out an arrangement of a song written by Doug Ward, their drummer. The number featured a guitar solo for Cary, which took all his concentration so that he didn't even notice Jane and Andy come in and sit down. This was kind of fun for Jane. It meant she got to look at him when he wasn't looking back at her, wasn't even aware that she was around.

It was a different view of him, watching him with the other guys in the band. He was more easygoing with them, kidding around between numbers. And he didn't seem bothered by any of their teasing. Like when he suggested incorporating some old sixties songs into one of their sets and Doug said, "Then we'll have to get a sixties name for the group."

"Yeah," said Dennis Allen, the keyboard player, "Like Cary and the Paramedics."

"We could all wear white jackets and stethoscopes," added Harvey Sims, the bass guitarist.

"Okay, okay," Cary said, putting his arms up over his head, as if protecting himself from stuff they were throwing at him. "I give. Back to the present. Long live New Wave!"

At first Jane felt hurt. If *she'd* teased Cary like that, he would have really bristled. But then she realized it was probably because he cared a lot about what she thought, especially what she thought of *him*. She smiled slightly at this idea, and watched from the shadows as Cary sang the lead on the next number, backing away from the mike to play his guitar, leaning way in toward it for each line he sang.

She loved the reedy sound of his voice. Sometimes when they were alone, he'd pick out songs on his old acoustic guitar and sing just for her. She always carried little memories of these private performances with her when she heard him with the band, and it always gave her a kind of thrill to hear him sing for hundreds when she knew he'd do it all just for her alone. A concert for one.

Just then, as she was smiling about Cary, the dark recess where she and Andy were sitting came alive with lights: red, blue, green, white in waves, and then pulsing all at once.

"Matt," Andy said, then started laughing. "I think he's trying to get our attention."

"You mean *your* attention," Jane said, pinching Andy in the ribs to show her she knew what was going on.

This sudden light show was less appreciated by the band.

"Hey, Matt, what's going on back there? Did you drop a dog onto the light board?" Cary shouted back. Then he looked in the direction where all the lights were focused, and saw Jane and Andy. He broke into a wide grin.

"All right," he told the rest of the band, holding up his hand, "why don't we take five. We seem to have some visitors. Being the sociable guy that I am, I'll take it upon myself to welcome them."

And with that, he propped his guitar against one of the amps and came over to give Jane a big hug.

"So, she dragged you along to be tortured by our dismal practicing," he said to Andy.

"Actually, you don't sound half bad," Andy told him, then seeing Matt Hall walking across the room toward them, added, "but your lighting needs some work. Seems a little on the psychedelic side."

Matt grinned shyly and said, "I was trying to get your attention."

"Well, you succeeded," Andy said, smiling back. "Trouble was you destroyed everyone else's."

When the two of them had gone off so Matt could show her his light board, Jane had Cary alone for a minute, which was what she'd been waiting for. She had lain awake the night before thinking and thinking about Alison's wedding. She knew Neal would love to come in from Boston for it. He would really like knowing he was Jane's choice to go with her to such an obviously important event. He loved to dress up for formal occasions. Plus he was a great dancer, and there was supposed to be dancing at the reception. All in all, Neal would be great at a wedding. He was so clean-cut and socially smooth.

Cary, on the other hand, would probably insist on coming in his leather jacket and sunglasses. His nod to the formality of the occasion would probably be to wear a *gold* stud in his ear instead of the usual silver one. In so many ways, Cary was just the most dreadfully wrong person to invite to Alison's wedding. The problem was that he was the one she really wanted to bring.

And so she had, by two-thirty in the morning, finally reached the decision to disappoint Neal, and let Cary know she wanted him to be her date. She still felt kind of rotten about this, offering him something that would mean so much to someone else, but she also knew she had to follow her heart. If she invited Neal just because she thought she should, she'd probably wind up being awful to him all night. No, she would let Cary be her date.

What she hadn't considered during all her hours of tossing and turning and pondering in the dark the night before, was that Cary might have other ideas.

"Huh?" was his initial response to her invitation.

"I said would you like to be my date for Alison's wedding?"

"Oh, Jane, you've got to be kidding. I'd rather play marathon Parcheesi than go to a wedding. I mean, what a total waste of time."

She wished she were holding a big cream pie so she could mash it in his smug, rebellious face. In this fantasy, she'd take his sunglasses off first, then put them back on over the whipped cream.

But as it was, she had no pie and no snappy comeback to his little speech, and so all she could do was be a complete wimp and start to cry. She ran out of the room, up the stairs, and out onto the road leading back to Canby Hall.

She heard footsteps running hard behind her. Hoping they belonged to a sorry Cary, she turned. It was Andy.

"Hey, girl, wait up," she shouted. And then when she had caught up with Jane, she said breathlessly, "What's wrong?"

"What's wrong?" Jane said. "Oh, nothing. I've just got the most difficult boyfriend of the century. Plus I've got absolutely no cool, no polish, no scathing wit, no drop-em-in-their-tracks looks. Boy, sometimes I can't wait to be twenty-five."

"I'll help. I can teach you a great drop-em-in-their-tracks look by tomorrow. I learned that sort of thing early. As for the difficult boyfriend, he'll probably come around."

"Well, you know," Jane said, thinking out loud, "I'm not entirely sure I'm going to let him."

CHAPTER FIVE

After that last beautiful Sunday, the skies turned gray and the winds cool. Fall descended on Canby Hall. The next three weeks rushed by in a flurry of Halloween parties, then midterms, and the fall choral concert, and suddenly it was nearly Thanksgiving. Ordinarily, most of the girls would have gone home, or off with friends for the long weekend. But this year, nearly every girl in Baker planned to stay at school. None of them wanted to miss a moment of the excitement surrounding Alison's wedding.

Alison herself was getting a little edgy, both from being on the verge of such a big step in her life, and from being the focus of so much attention. She found herself grateful for the few moments of peace and quiet she could usually find at the end of her days.

Tuesday night after sign-in and bed check,

she climbed the narrow old staircase to the top floor of Baker House. There under the ivy-covered eaves was her attic loft, nicknamed "The Penthouse" by her three favorite old girls, the former occupants of 407, Dana, Faith, and Shelley. A wave of nostalgia swept over her when she thought about them — about the fun and all the adventures and all the scrapes they'd had while they were at Canby Hall. (And Alison had a feeling that she only knew about half of the adventures and scrapes.) Nostalgia gave way to a little rush of excitement at the thought of how soon she'd be seeing them again. All three of them were due in tomorrow, from very different directions. Faith was flying in from Rochester, New York, where she was studying photography at the university. Shelley was flying from the state university in Iowa, where she was majoring in drama. Dana, who was taking a year off between high school and college, spending time with her father, was flying in from Hawaii.

Alison was excited to see them, but a little nervous about what they'd all think of David. When the three of them had graduated last June, Alison had been very involved with Michael. She knew Dana, Faith, and Shelley all liked him a lot and thought they were a great match. David was so different from Michael. Would they be able to accept him?

David. Just thinking about him made Alison's heart do a little thumping thing inside her. She could actually feel it. And she just knew that at this very moment he was thinking about her, too. The emotions and connections between her and David were so strong that, when she pushed open the door to The Penthouse and heard the phone ringing, she knew it was him. It was almost like telepathy. It worked the other way, too.

Whenever she called him, he picked up the receiver and said, "Hi, Alison."

Picking up the phone in The Penthouse, though, first necessitated *finding* it amid the higher-than-usual level of rubble. Finally, on the sixth ring, she tracked it down beneath a pile of running sweats and shoes. She dove for it and picked up the receiver.

"Hi, David."

"Hi," he said in a way Alison loved. She couldn't possibly explain this to anyone. She'd feel like an idiot trying to tell someone how he managed to put so much meaning into those two little letters, that one syllable . . . "Hi."

She curled up against one of the big floor pillows she had scattered around the living room and talked with him about the day they'd each had. Since meeting David, one of her favorite parts of any day was talking to him about it just before she went to sleep.

Doby the cat could tell how happy she was now. He came across the floor, purring, and then pressed his little head against her shoulder and fell asleep.

Just when the conversation was getting to a good part — David was telling her what had attracted him to her that first night they'd met, at a big party they'd both hated — there came a soft tap tap tap on her door.

"Argh," she whispered into the receiver. "As much as I love being a housemother, there are certain moments when I wish it weren't such a twenty-four-hour-a-day job. At this hour, it's probably somebody in a crisis of some kind. It might be a broken heart, or an F on a midterm, or just a lost pet turtle, but I'd better get off and find out."

"Love you," David Gordon said from Boston.

"Ditto," Alison said, then put the receiver down as softly as she could, so it was as little like hanging up as possible. She hated hanging up from calls with David.

She went quietly to the door, and opened it to find three girls she didn't recognize. Actually, their own mothers could not have recognized them like this. Their hair was wrapped up in towel turbans, their faces covered in some kind of green mud pack. They were wearing old robes. Something about the robes was vaguely familiar to Alison. She tried to think. She prided herself on knowing all her Baker girls by name. This was especially important if they were at her door with a problem.

One of the girls spoke in a small odd voice, like a cartoon character.

"We were . . . uh . . . we were putting on this herbal beauty mask stuff, you know, and then we went down to the fourth floor washroom and the water's off!"

"The water's off?" Alison repeated, stalling for time. Something about the girl's voice was funny, and something about her robe was getting *very* familiar. It was a tradition at Canby Hall — not the kind of tradition Patrice Allardyce promoted, but an informal tradition among the students — for a girl to wear the same robe all the way through Canby Hall. And given the amount of time the girls spent in their robes around the dorm studying and gossiping and playing records and playing Hearts, the average robe was a pretty ratty item by graduation day. These robes had that really ratty look. So these girls must be seniors. But there were only a few seniors in Baker, and Alison knew them all well. So who were these mystery girls?

All of a sudden she had an inkling. She leaned out into the hallway and peered more closely at them. From inside the dried masks she saw three sets of impishly laughing eyes. One set of green eyes, one set of blue, one set of brown. And at the very instant that she was realizing who was inside these disguises, she was ambushed with hugs from them. It was Dana, Faith, and Shelley!

"Surprise!" they all shouted at once.

"B-b-but, how . . . I thought you were supposed to . . ." Alison sputtered.

"Well, we just *told* you we were coming on Wednesday morning. Do you believe everything you hear?" said the girl in the red robe. When she took the towel off her head and long brown hair tumbled down, Alison knew it was Dana.

"Actually," said the second girl, whose blond curls revealed that she was Shelley, "we all met in Boston this afternoon, had a great Chinese lunch, and plotted how we were going to fool you."

"But you figured us out, didn't you?" said Faith who, when she pulled off her towel, showed that she had changed her hairstyle from the afro Alison remembered to corn row braids with gold bands around the ends. "What clued you in?"

"Well," Alison said with a smile, "I don't think anyone in the history of the school ever managed to so thoroughly destroy their robes as you three did. I think it was the stuffing coming out of that particularly awful chartreuse satin quilted number of yours, Shel. I remember the first time I saw you in it, at a Sunday brunch. I recall wondering if could eat an omelet while looking at something that color. And hoping it wouldn't make it past the end of sophomore year."

"But with real perserverance, I managed to make it all the way through to graduation with a few shreds still intact," Shelley said, laughing.

Then in a tone of mock indignation she added, "I'll have you know I had to go all the way home last weekend and *beg* my mother to let me take this out of her rag bag and bring it out with me. Faith called me and told me to make sure and bring it. If we were going back to Canby Hall, we had to have our robes."

"I guess I'd better ask you in," Alison said. "If I were really mean, I'd make you wear those mud packs the rest of the night. Just for making me sweat there, trying to figure out which of my poor woebegone Baker girls you were. But seeing as I'm such a softy, I'll get you some wet towels so you can wipe that stuff off. Do you think it made you all more beautiful?" She led the three of them in. Doby, who had awakened and been scared off by the mud packs, came out of hiding, recognizing their voices, purring, and looking for some attention. Faith picked him up.

"Doby, old buddy. How's it been going? I hear your mistress has gone and fallen in love . . . with a capital L."

Alison, bringing the towels out from the kitchen, blushed.

"Oh, no," Dana teased, "it's worse than we thought."

"Oh, it *is*," Alison said. "Much worse. I never knew I could feel this way about anyone."

"That's wonderful. But what about Michael?" asked Shelley, who could always be counted on to ask the questions everyone else was too cool to ask. "Didn't you love *him*?"

Alison grew flustered.

"Of course I did. Yes. Well, not exactly. Not like this. Oh, I don't know. Don't ask me questions I can't answer. Just come in the kitchen with me and I'll put on some coffee. I'm going to need a little caffeine if we're going to be up all night talking."

And they were. They talked about what they were doing now. Shelley had gotten the lead in her school's production of *Hedda Gabler*. Faith was going to be featured in a student photography show at a gallery in Manhattan. Dana had been writing poetry and learning to surf.

"I'm not sure which is harder," she said.

They talked about old times, too. About all the problems they'd had in the process of becoming friends.

"I thought I was going to have to rent an umpire for a while there," Alison said.

"But you have to admit," Faith said, "that

once we got our act together, wild horses couldn't tear us apart."

"That's true," Alison said, handing Dana a package of cookies from the cabinet. "I must say I never knew a set of roommates who were as close as you. Although — this is interesting — the three girls who took over 407 look like they might be picking up your old spirit."

Dana nodded. She couldn't talk at first because of the cookie in her mouth. When she could, she said, "We left that spirit behind. It's a friendly old poltergeist named Lucy. She probably got those girls together. We'll have to go down and meet them tomorrow. Make sure they're keeping the old room in shape."

"Uh, well . . ." Alison said, pouring out four mugs of coffee, and shooing Doby off the counter where he was trying to get into the carton of milk. "I think they've made a few changes. Minor ones, of course," she lied.

CHAPTER SIX

The night up at Alison's turned out to be a pajama party, with the four old friends awake until nearly four, catching up on all the months they hadn't seen each other. Dana, Faith, and Shelley slept in until nearly noon the next day, then showered and dressed, and decided their first stop just had to be their old room. When they got there, though, they were in for a few surprises. Faith, having seen the room weeks before, was prepared.

"Oh, no!" Dana exclaimed as they stood in front of the open door to 407, looking in. "Where did our room go?"

"Maybe we're on the wrong floor," Shelley said.

"No," said Faith, stepping back to check, "it says 407 right here on the door. But these turkeys have really done the place over. I didn't have the heart to tell you."

"Yeah," said Dana, "where did our old Black Hole disappear to? I can understand that black walls might not be everyone's idea of the ultimate decor, but this pukey blue, well, as we used to say in French class — *Donnez-moi un break!*"

"Well," Shelley said with a chuckle, "at least we gave them a bit of trouble. I'll bet that black was a real challenge to paint over. They probably had to give it six coats of whatever you call this yucky color."

" 'Wedgwood Blue,' " said an icy voice from behind them. It was Jane, back from morning classes. "Now, if you'll excuse me, this is my room and I'd like to get into it." She brushed past them roughly as she came in.

"Oh, Jane. Hi," Dana said.

Jane turned and said, "Hello, Dana." She and Jane had been in the Canby Hall chorale the year before and so knew each other a little.

"What did you do to our floor islands?" Shelley asked her.

"If you are referring to the mattresses on the floor, we decided against your 'gangster hideout' motif. We found the old bed frames down in the basement and put the mattresses back on them. As you can see, I have an antique quilt. It is for a bed, not a *floor island*. Also, it goes with 'Wedgwood Blue,' which happens to be my favorite color."

In spite of the tension of the moment, or maybe because of it, Faith started giggling.

She pointed to the tea bag hanging from the ceiling over one of the beds.

"Doesn't that clash a little with 'Wedgwood Blue'? Or does it have some deep significance that I'm missing?"

"You'd have to ask my roommate Toby. It's her tea bag, and her business as to why she hung it up there."

Jane was bluffing. No one, not even she and Andy, knew why Toby had hung a tea bag from the ceiling above her bed. She'd done it the day she arrived all silent and surly from Texas, taken it down when she'd planned to run away, and stuck it back up when she had decided to stay. In the months since, she had ducked all questions about its meaning. By now, it had become one of the minor mysteries of Baker House.

Jane closed this subject, as well as any further conversation, by saying, "If you'll excuse me, I have a biology midterm in sixth period. I'm already going to have to skip lunch to cram for it, so I really don't have any time to answer prying questions." With that, she sat down at her desk and opened her text.

Faith, Dana, and Shelley exchanged silent looks, shrugging their shoulders to indicate that none of them knew quite what to do now. They all knew they'd been hopelessly cloddish, but couldn't think how to retrace their steps. Finally Dana, the socially smoothest of the three, took the lead, stepping into the room a little, addressing Jane.

"Ummm," she said, and cleared her throat. Eventually, Jane looked up and Dana pressed on. "I think maybe we didn't get off to the absolutely best start here. I'd like to try again. Faith and Shelley and I used to live in this room. We've got a lot of memories tied up here, and we were just stopping by to check the old place out. I apologize if we stepped on your toes."

"Apology accepted," Jane said coldly, and went straight back to her book.

"Do you think we could go in?" Shelley whispered. "I'd kind of like to look under the bookcase and see if my initials are still there."

"Not now, Shel," Faith said, giving her friend's sleeve a light tug, moving their conversation out into the hallway. "We didn't do too great at this. We should probably just come back another time."

"Let's catch Maggie on her way back from classes," Dana suggested. "I barely got to talk with her last night before she put the mud packs on us. We could all go over to the dining hall together for lunch."

"Oh, no," Faith said. "Not me. I'm not nearly ready for Canby Hall cuisine. Actually, I was kind of hoping to be able to make it through the whole weekend on machine food and pizza, plus a daily Snickers supplement, of course." She pulled one out of her pocket. "But you two go on. I'll meet you after lunch. I'll just go down to the Ping-Pong room machines and get a Tab to go with this."

"A balanced meal," Dana said sarcastically.

"Yeah, yeah, Hawaii girl," Faith teased back, "you've been living on pineapple and sunshine these past months while I've been in my cave developing pictures. Basically, I'm into the photographer's diet — foods that are easy to eat in the dark."

Down at the machines in the Ping-Pong room, where the girls in Baker made it a reverse point of coolness to *never* play Ping-Pong, Faith found herself in line at the soda machine behind another black girl, who was having trouble getting the old rattletrap machine to work. She'd slip in her quarters at the top and they'd slip right out into the coin return in the bottom. After watching her go through this exasperating process twice, Faith interrupted.

"Excuse me. Maybe I can help."

The girl turned around and smiled broadly at Faith. "Faith Thompson?" she asked.

Faith smiled back at the girl in recognition.

The girl said, "Remember me? Andrea Cord. We met last month when you were here."

Faith nodded. "Of course I remember. You

were upset about not getting the lead in the ballet."

Andy looked down at her hands in embarrassment. "Well, I guess you were right about that. It wasn't because of my color. The other girl *was* better, but . . . ." Andy stopped and gazed at the soda machine.

Faith, aware of Andy's embarrassment, took the girl's quarters, dropped one in, and quickly kicked the machine in its midsection. Then she dropped the second quarter in and pounded the machine on its side.

Then she turned to the girl and asked, "What kind of soda are you trying to get out of Godzilla here?"

"Well, I was kind of hoping for a root beer, but at this point I'd take anything," Andy said.

Faith gave the root beer button four hard thumps with the bottom of her fist and kicked the machine again — "for good luck," she told the girl — and the can came thudding through. Faith pulled it out and turned and handed it to Andy with a wide grin.

"Girl — One. Machine — Zero," she said. "An old trick. One of the pieces of my education that'll probably stay with me for the rest of my life. Years after I've forgotten the chemical symbol for lead, I'll be able to come back here and make this machine cough up a can of soda."

Seconds after Faith had put her karate moves on the machine, the doorway to the Ping-Pong room was suddenly filled with Patrice Allardyce and a tall, severe-looking young woman in a dark suit and sensible oxfords.

"Yes," Ms. Allardyce was saying, "here's one of our lovely recreational facilities, the Ping-Pong room. Oh, how I love to come by and hear the tiny clop-clop of the ball and the lilting laughter of girls joyously involved in sport!"

"Hmmm," said the young woman, who was surely a candidate for Alison's job. "Actually I don't believe in too much recreation for adolescent girls. The school where I last worked had a more structured format. Instead of free time or recreation periods, we added language lab sessions and computer courses and extra study halls." She stopped here and smiled, then went on. "So even if they could find a moment to get into mischief, they were too exhausted to even think about it."

When Ms. Allardyce had led the candidate out of the Ping-Pong room and down the hall toward the laundry room, the girls could hear the young woman saying, "At my old school we also sometimes had early evening classes."

The two girls looked at each other and rolled their eyes. When they felt safely alone again, Faith said, "I wonder where that school of hers was located — Devil's Island?"

"But what if P.A. hires her?" Andy moaned.

"Oh, don't worry. P.A. may be strict, but she also loves all the pomp and pageantry and high spiritedness of Canby Hall. If she hired the Enforcer here, well, the annual Leaf Rake would turn into an ecological seminar on mulch and compost heaps. Someone like that would take all the fun out of everything. Don't worry. You won't get anyone as great as Alison, but you probably won't get this woman, either."

"Maggie Morrison told us you and Dana and Shelley were coming in last night to surprise Alison. I'm glad you're here. Especially you. You know why."

"Why?" Faith asked.

"Oh, come on," Andy said. "Things can't have changed that much since you graduated. You mean to tell me you didn't feel a little . . . well . . . on the outside when you were here?"

Faith thought for a long moment, then shook her head from side to side. "No, I can't honestly say I did. But what I'm hearing is that *you* do." Faith tossed her head a little, sending a ripple through her weighted braids. Andy thought Faith looked incredibly sophisticated in her parachute pants and jacket with spaceman shoulders — very art-school. Usually she felt very hip and trendy herself, but next to Faith she felt like a kid playing dress-up. Three years really made a difference when they were the ones between fifteen and eighteen. Faith was a young woman and she, Andy, was still a girl. Which was precisely how Faith was treating her. And it was making her furious. Suddenly she wanted to score a few points off Faith Thompson.

"Are you going to tell me that everyone around here was blind to the fact that you're black, that they treated you exactly like they would've if you were a white girl?"

Faith thought about this, hiking herself up onto the dusty, never-used Ping-Pong table. She started smiling at a thought that crossed her mind.

"Well, I *do* remember the day before we were having our graduation pictures taken, and there was a slip in everybody's mailbox, telling them what time to show up and where. And at the bottom, it said not to wear a white blouse or sweater. I'll tell you I puzzled over that one for a good long while and then I handed the sheet to Dana. She read it and said, 'Doesn't apply to you, Faith. They want some contrast between our faces and our clothes. So a white shirt's okay for you.' Oh, sure, Andy, at the beginning I felt outside — even with Dana and Shelley — but then I really felt at home."

"You can't be serious," Andy said, sitting down on the old linoleum floor facing Faith. "I feel different every day around here. Back home in Chicago, practically everyone I knew was black. I hardly ever gave my color a thought. Around here, I'm forced to think about it all the time. I feel like the odd girl out, like everyone's looking at me to see what black girls do. Last weekend, I was putting on some blush in the girls' john at the Oakley Prep dance, and some girl I don't even know is looking over my shoulder real amazed and she says, 'Oh, wow, I didn't know they had makeup for you.' "

"What did you say to that?" Faith asked.

"Well, I told her black makeup was actually very rare because black girls are so good-looking they hardly need any."

Faith burst out laughing, and said, "All *right*. But what about your close white friends? You don't think they see you as different, do you?"

"No, not my roommates. They see me as Andy first and black second, or maybe tenth, or maybe not at all. They're great. But there are other girls. This Gigi Norton who used to live with my roommate Jane. . . ."

"Oh, no! Gigi Norton! I remember her. Sort of like I remember this soda machine. You can't use her as an example. She's terrible to everyone. She makes blimp remarks to fat girls, beanpole jokes to skinny ones, and asks the tall girls how the weather is up there. She's just a walking insult machine, and not a typical Canby Hall girl."

"I'm not saying this is a hotbed of prejudice. Just that white girls, especially when there's a lot of them together, have a way of making a black girl feel *very* different."

"Then things *have* changed since I was here," Faith said.

"Or maybe you've just forgotten what it was *really* like," Andy said, getting up off the floor, finishing her root beer, and tossing the can into the wastebasket on her way out. Just before she got to the door, she turned back to Faith and said, "You've been a long time in a white world now. Maybe what happens is you start to lose your blackness a little. Maybe you start to go a little *beige*."

After lunch, Maggie, who'd just finished midterms that morning, wanted to celebrate by dyeing her hair. She asked Dana to help. And so the Morrison sisters headed for the fourth floor washroom of Baker, where Maggie intended to transform her mousy brown tresses to a color called "Blue Lagoon."

"That can't really be the name of the color," Dana said as they walked down the hall, arms loaded with towels and shampoo and the coloring kit Maggie had bought the day before. She picked up the box and read the label for Dana.

"Yep. Blue Lagoon. It was the most interesting shade I could find in the whole drugstore. I'm sick of being everybody's favorite goofy-looking kid. I'm going to make a dramatic entrance into Alison's wedding. Nobody'll recognize me. They'll all just turn and whisper, 'Who's that exotic, mysterious new girl?' "

"I don't know about this," Dana said. "It seems like an iffy proposition. And get the box out of sight! If Alison sees it, she'll be furious. As I remember, dyeing — clothes or hair or anything — was the one thing she was an absolute fiend against."

"Still is," Maggie said, tucking the box into the stack of old towels. "She says it leaves the john a disaster area. But I'm going to be incredibly careful. I mean, if it were such a mess, how could they sell millions of these kits? You just have to do it right. Here. See. You just use this handy applicator to spread on the activating color foam after you mix it with the highlighting crystals. I mean, look at the picture on the box here. See, this woman is using it, and she's all neat and tidy. There's just a little of this foam on her head. Sort of like styling mousse."

Half an hour later, Toby Houston, back from her American lit midterm, came into the washroom to find three sinks, a six-foot patch of floor, and the two Morrison sisters covered in blue-black gunk.

"Oh, wow! What happened? Did the sewer back up? I'll go get Alison," she said, trying to be helpful.

"DON'T!!" shouted Dana and Maggie in unison. Then, hearing the terror in their own voices, they realized how ridiculous they must look to Toby. Which sent them into a wave of helpless laughter.

"Are you guys okay?" Toby asked.

"I'm not sure," Maggie said. "We started out dyeing my hair. We seem to be also dyeing Dana and this bathroom in the process. We've gone out of control is what's happened."

"You haven't seen Alison around here, have you?" Dana asked nervously. "Please say you haven't. She'll kill us if she sees this mess."

"I did see her, but you don't have to worry. She was walking through the lobby, and she didn't look like she had dorm problems on her mind. She was walking with David. It was pretty interesting . . . two people managing to walk across a lobby with that many arms around each other."

"You know, I've yet to see this David Gordon," Dana said, trying to rub some of the dye off her hands with one of the towels.

"*Very* cute," Maggie said.

"Of course, we don't really know him," Toby said. "I guess the important thing, though, is that Alison's sold on him."

"Yeah, I know she is," Dana said, "but I wonder if it's *real*. I mean, how can she be so sure after only a month or two?"

"Don't you believe in love at first sight?" asked Maggie from underneath the tap of rushing water, where she was trying to get the dye out. This didn't seem to be happening, though. The water kept running dark blue. Dana came over to help out, scrubbing her sister's head under the faucet.

"I believe in *attraction* at first sight," she said. "But I think love is something that has to grow. I think Alison's been swept off her feet by his glamorous tv personality, and isn't thinking straight." She toweled Maggie's head, then started wiping off the sinks and mirror.

Maggie plugged in her blow dryer and started fluffing out her hair.

"Are you sure we got all the dye out?" she asked Dana. "It looks awful, awful blue to me."

"The water was clear at the end. I think what's in there is yours to keep. Like it or not."

When Maggie was done, the three of them stood in front of the mirror, all thinking pretty much the same thing. Toby was the first to say it. She was kind and goodhearted, but absolutely unable to tell a lie.

"Boy, Maggie. No offense, but you sure look weird."

"It does look pretty strange," Maggie admitted. "Kind of like a cheap wig."

"Maybe if you wash it a few times, the color will come out," Dana said hopefully.

Maggie shook her head sorrowfully while eyeing herself in the mirror.

"Nope. I made sure and got the permanent kind of color."

"Maybe you could get your hair cut," Toby suggested.

"Why?" Maggie said despairingly. "Then I'd just look like I was wearing a *short* cheap wig. No, I think I'm just going to have to get a hat for Alison's wedding."

"If that smear across your forehead is also indelible," Dana said, "I'd make that a hat with a *veil*."

CHAPTER SEVEN

Thanksgiving morning, Dana woke up from a dream of lying on the sunny deck of a sailboat. When she opened her eyes, she realized that the sun was not high overhead, but streaming in through the windows of Alison's apartment, and that the deck was the floor of Alison's living room. The *hard* floor of Alison's living room. Too many of the muscles in Dana's body were aching from a night spent on this floor. The night before, she and Faith and Shelley had drawn straws for who would get Alison's guest futon. Faith and Shelley had won for the second night in a row. Dana looked across the room at them. They were still sleeping. *They* were probably having dreams of lying on a nice soft cloud.

Dana sat up and stretched. That felt better. She fished around in the pile of dropped clothes at her feet and found her watch. It was only seven-fifteen. No matter. She knew she wasn't going to get back to sleep no matter how early it was, and so she might as well get her running shoes on and go out for a run.

She slipped out of The Penthouse and down the stairs, out onto the campus where the dry leaves on the ground were being stirred up into the air by gusty winds. Luckily, she had worn her sweats and a quilted vest. She'd be warm enough, even on a long run . . . even on a run all the way out to the Crowell horse farm.

As soon as she thought this, Dana wondered how long it had been lurking in the back of her mind. Probably since she arrived at Canby Hall. The odd thing was, she wasn't sure *why* she wanted to see Randy again. They'd split up long before she'd graduated. Whatever had happened between them had ended long ago. Still. Just because you break up with someone doesn't mean you erase them completely from your mind, she thought. She just wanted to see how Randy was doing. What was wrong with that?

She ran at a steady, easy pace, her long, dark brown hair sprayed out behind her by the wind. Dana loved to run — in Manhattan where she came from, in Hawaii where she was now living, but especially here in the low rolling hills of Massachusetts. From having run these country roads for three years, she knew them by heart, and loved them with all her heart. She saw all the old familiar landmarks on the way to Randy's — the old one-room Colonial schoolhouse with its tiny dollhouse of a library out back, the Wilbers' grazing land with its little white cloud of sheep, and the massive old oak tree where Randy had carved a small heart with their initials inside. She stopped at the tree. The heart was still there, along with the initials of a dozen other couples. She wondered how many of the paired initials on the side of this old tree belonged to people who no longer knew each other.

This thought — of lost love, of times past and gone forever, of this place she'd left behind — started her crying. And even when she started running again, the tears wouldn't stop. The wind rushing against her cheeks just pushed the tears back to where her hair started in fine tendrils. It took her nearly the whole way to Randy's place to pull herself together.

When she got close, she stopped on a ridge overlooking the farm. A thin wisp of smoke was coming out of the stack at the side of the house. Randy's mother still cooked on the old woodburning stove that had been in the kitchen since the house was built in the early 1800's. She probably already had a big turkey in the oven for the family's Thanksgiving dinner.

Dana hesitated for a moment. If she turned back now, everything between her and Randy would stay neatly pressed like a rose in a scrapbook. If she went down there, her story with Randy would have a new chapter. Did she really want that?

She never had a chance to decide. Before she could run down to the house, or turn back, she heard hard heavy hoofbeats behind her. She turned and, sure enough, there was Randy.

She smiled as soon as she saw him. He had always looked so great on a horse. Riding was almost more natural to him than walking. And it was good to see that he hadn't changed all that much. He was still wearing the oldest pair of Levi's in America, and still had that great straw cowboy hat with the brim bent so far down in front it was a wonder he could see past his nose.

She waved at him. He kept coming toward her, but didn't wave back. As he got closer, Dana could see that there was no smile on his face to match hers. He rode to within a few feet of where she stood and reined his horse up sharply.

"Hello, Dana," he said coldly.

"Hi," she said back, and then, trying to lighten things up a little, added, "I was just in the neighborhood and thought I'd stop by."

"Hear you're living in Hawaii these days," he said. He was just being polite. She could tell.

"Yeah. For a year. With my dad and Eve and their baby. I'm getting a lot of practice surfing and baby-sitting a one-year-old. Actually, I kind of like having a little time off to loaf before I go to college." She felt so dumb, standing here chattering on in the face of what looked like complete lack of interest from Randy. She tried to get him to say something. "So, how's it going with you?"

"Can't complain," he said.

Dana waited for more, but there wasn't any. She remembered how silent he could be.

"Well, I guess I'll get on with my run," she said, since there didn't seem to be anything else to say. "My old route took me by here and I just had to stop for a minute to see the farm. Good seeing you, Randy." She started off.

"Wait," she heard from behind her. She stopped and turned around and caught something intense in Randy's eyes. She couldn't tell whether it was intense-good or intense-bad. He slid out of his saddle, dropped to the ground, and said, "If you don't mind slowing down for a while, I'll walk you a ways."

"Oh," Dana said, surprised at his change of heart. "Sure."

"So," he said when they were walking side by side through a field of drying wild flowers, "you're in for Alison's wedding."

"How'd you know about the wedding? Your birds and squirrels tell you?" It was an old joke, about how much time he spent outside, close to the trees and animals, away from people.

"Well, I'm not quite as out of touch with civilization as you always thought I was," he answered mysteriously.

Dana thought about this remark. If he knew about Alison's wedding, he probably heard it from some girl at Canby Hall. Which probably meant he was involved with someone there. A senior maybe. But who? Then she stopped herself. It was none of her business.

It was odd. On the surface, thinking that Randy might have a new girl friend made her happy for him. But somewhere underneath — and this kind of surprised her — Dana felt a twinge of jealousy. And so she didn't ask him specifically where he'd heard about Alison. And she noticed that he didn't ask her about her social life in Hawaii. Maybe he didn't care if she was involved with someone there (she was, but only sort of). Or maybe he wasn't asking because he cared *too* much. Not knowing what was going on in his head piqued Dana's interest. It added an element of flirtation to the conversation. Harmless flirtation, she thought. After all, he knew she was only here for the wedding. He couldn't think that anything real or serious could start up between them in one weekend.

They walked and talked for a while, away from the farm and his family, off on their own. And when he draped an arm over her shoulder, as they went through a grove of low-branched maple trees, she thought, Well, what's the harm? He's just being friendly and gallant. But then, when they got deep into the maple grove and he leaned over to kiss her, Dana backed off sharply.

"Uh, Randy . . ." she started to say, but didn't have time to finish. He looked at her as if she'd slapped him, and then got up onto his horse and rode off as fast as he could, given that he practically had to lie across his horse's neck to clear the trees on the way out of the grove.

Dana called after him, but he didn't, or wouldn't, hear her.

When he'd disappeared from sight, Dana sat down on a fallen tree and thought for a while. She wasn't sure what had gone wrong. She didn't really think she'd been leading him on, just fooling around.

She sighed and got up and started back toward Canby Hall, walking. She didn't have it in her to run anymore this morning. When she reached the old highway, she was surprised to see Toby Houston coming from the direction of school. Odd that she'd be out this way so early in the morning, especially on a holiday, when she could sleep in.

They exchanged hi's and then Dana asked Toby where she was headed. She didn't mean it to be a troublesome question, but it clearly was. Toby grew flustered and said, "Oh, I'm just paying a visit to a friend. Lives out this way."

Dana noted that Toby didn't use any personal pronoun, didn't indicate whether the friend was a he or a she. Hmmm. But no, Toby and Randy? No! She was too young for him!

When Toby first got to the horse barn, she couldn't find Randy. She looked in every stall, then finally climbed up into the hayloft and found him there, sitting in the corner, high on a stack of hay bales, looking miserable.

"Somebody die?" she asked.

Usually, she could joke him out of a bad mood. This time, though, he just looked at her like she was barely there. Like she was a see-through person. He held up a hand as if to keep her away and said, "Not now. I've got to be by myself for a while. I'll see you later. Okay?"

Toby nodded and backed down the ladder. One of the main features of their friendship was that they respected each other's moods. But this time she couldn't help wishing she could be there to help him out of it. She also couldn't help wondering what had brought it on.

Or who, she thought, when she put together the facts of Dana on the road coming from this direction and what she knew about Randy's susceptibility to his old girl friend. She hoped Dana wasn't causing Randy any trouble.

She stopped along the roadside, spread her hands flat on the top of a fencepost, set her chin down, and looked out over a just-harvested wheat field. She tried to sort out her feelings about her and Randy and Dana. It was funny in a way. Although she was only fifteen, and practically the most socially in-experienced girl at Canby Hall, here she was feeling protective of a twenty-year-old guy who treated her like a kid sister.

And it was funny, too, that she felt protective rather than jealous. She just didn't want Dana to hurt Randy. Also, she didn't want Dana to turn out to be a bad person. She wanted to like her. After all, she was Maggie's sister and Alison's friend.

Still, if she's rotten to Randy, I'll just have to punch her lights out, Toby thought, then burst out laughing at herself and her Texas temper. She'd have to cool that down a little if she was going to last at Canby Hall. That wasn't how they did things here. This wasn't the Harmon County Junior Rodeo where she'd socked Larry Burrell in the jaw after he expressed the opinion that girls shouldn't be allowed to ride in rodeos because they were wimps.

She smiled with satisfaction recalling the

right she'd landed on Larry. But that was there, and this was here. If Dana was being bad to Randy, Toby would just have to come up with some sophisticated, civilized, well-behaved equivalent of punching her lights out.

CHAPTER EIGHT

The three old roommates — Shelley, Faith, and Dana — made a pact to squeeze into the long weekend all the things they had liked doing best at Canby Hall.

One of these things was swimming in the school pool. Or rather fooling around in the school pool. Shelley was the one real swimmer among them. She'd been on teams since junior high, and now swam women's junior varsity at Iowa. Faith and Dana were sloggers in the water. Neither of them could win in a race against a turtle, but they could keep themselves afloat and in (more or less) forward motion from one end of the pool to the other. Usually when the three of them swam together, Shelley watched and gave the other two pointers. Which they usually forgot by the next time they came to the pool. Shelley had long ago despaired of ever turning her two friends into aquatic beings.

Since it was Thursday, Thanksgiving Day, with most of the student body home eating turkey, the three of them had the pool to themselves. Or at least Faith and Dana did. They'd been standing around in the shallow end for ten minutes now, gossiping about David Gordon, whom they'd seen coming to pick up Alison that morning. The other thing they were doing was waiting for Shelley.

"Where *is* that girl?" Faith said. "We're going to get waterlogged if she doesn't show up soon. She doesn't care if we drown without her."

"I heard that," Shelley shouted, coming out of the locker room, tugging her rubber racing cap on over her short blond curls, "and I *do* care. I just got hung up in town."

"Did you find Tom?" Dana asked. Tom was Shelley's old boyfriend from her days at Canby Hall. After graduation, they had written each other for a while, but he had suddenly stopped writing a few months before. When last seen this morning, Shelley was heading for Greenleaf, determined to find out why.

"Oh, yeah," she said, sliding into the water next to them, "I found him all right. I went to his house and his mother informed me he'd gone for a walk with Cynthia."

"Who's *Cynthia!*?" Faith asked, pushing off the wall, doing a little of her specialty, what she called the "back frog stroke."

"That's what I wondered, so I decided to find them."

"You went looking for them?!" Faith asked, laughing. "Shel, you've got more nerve than all of us put together!"

"How'd you even know where to go looking?" Dana asked, now stretched out from the side of the pool, practicing her flutter kick.

"Oh," Shelley said, "I've been on enough romantic walks around here to know most of the routes that people in love take. Don't bend your knees so much when you kick, Dana."

"So where did you find them?" Faith asked.

"And how did you know they were in love?" Dana added, kicking so hard that Shelley jumped back a little, laughing.

"Well. A, I found them up around Meyers' Bluff. And B, I figured that if they weren't in love they were at least in heavy-duty 'like,' when I saw him giving her a little bouquet he'd made from wild flowers."

"Tom?! Mr. Sensible, making little wild-flower bouquets?" Faith was amazed. "I'd like to have gotten a picture of that."

"So of course you turned around and walked away," Dana said, bobbing up and down in the water now, doing a terrible parody of a water ballet.

"Are you kidding?" Shelley said, tossing her goggles into the water and jumping in after them. "I walked right up to them and waited while he introduced me to her. Her name's

Cynthia Sanders. She was wearing — I'm not kidding — little white socks with bunnies on them."

"No," Faith and Dana said in unison.

'It's true," Shelley said. "And she had on this little pink angora beret."

"Stop," Faith said, covering her ears. "Don't tell me any more."

"I have to," Shelley said. "I can't stop now. She was holding Tom's little finger with her little finger. She was calling him Tom-Tom. And the worst thing was how much he was loving all of it. He kept looking at her the whole time with this most awful goony look."

"Was he nice to you?" Dana wondered.

"Shy. He kept looking at the ground. He acted like we'd barely known each other. Like we'd been on the same volleyball team or something. He clearly did not want Snookums to know we'd dated for nearly three years. The rat."

"But you've got Paul back home in Pine Bluff," Faith consoled. "And you say you're dating this new guy at school. Mark. So how can you be mad that Tom's found a new girl friend?"

"Well, at least I'm not going out with someone who holds onto my little finger," Shelley said irrationally, then pushed off the wall into ten fast laps of freestyle. Faith and Dana stood watching her blow off steam.

"What's really got her so burned?" Dana

wondered aloud. "She hasn't seen Tom since we graduated. It can't be that she still cares for him."

"Oh, but it's a tricky business when they go for someone else. If the new girl is gorgeous and brilliant and rich and famous, it's depressing, because it looks like he's traded up. If she's wearing bunny socks, what does that say about his taste . . . *and* about you."

Their conversation was interrupted here by the clearly enunciated tones of Patrice Allardyce, made more clearly enunciated by the echo-chamber effect of the tiled, high-ceilinged pool room. She came in ushering a short, stocky, sturdy-looking young woman with strawlike hair.

"Our lovely new pool," Ms. Allardyce was saying, waving her hand in a broad sweep.

"You'd think she built it," Dana whispered to Faith.

"Sssh. Let's listen. She's giving the tour to another candidate for Alison's job."

"What a splendid athletic facility," the young woman said. "I'm a great believer in the philosophy, *'A healthy body. A healthy mind.'* Three or four hours of sports and exercise a day, I find, works wonders with teenage girls. They don't have time for superfluous activities like talking and snacking and napping and makeup and playing cards. And their heads are clearer for their studies."

"Three or four hours a day," Patrice Allardyce mused. "Isn't that rather a lot?"

"Oh, they don't like it much at first, but they can take it. I used to be a drill sergeant in a WAC boot camp and so I know what I'm talking about."

Faith and Dana bobbed underwater to keep themselves from laughing. By the time they surfaced, the visitors had gone.

"Oh, those poor Baker girls are really in for something. She was showing another one of these possible houseparents around yesterday, when I was down in the Ping-Pong room getting told off by Andy Cord," Faith said.

"Getting told off? What'd you do to her, cheat at Ping-Pong?"

"Dana. You know no one's ever played Ping-Pong at that table. No, she seems to think I'm not quite black enough, just because I said I hadn't felt weird around here. Well, you tell me — when we met, did you think I was weird because I'm black?"

Dana thought a moment, then said, "Because you're black . . . no. But weird . . . definitely!"

This statement, of course, got Dana a good dunking.

Shelley came to her rescue and splashed Faith away. This started a three-way water fight that lasted quite a while, took up the whole pool, and left all three of them collapsed in exhaustion and laughter by the time it was over.

* * *

Later, when they were in the locker room, drying their hair and dressing, Shelley said, "Anybody know what time it is?"

"Five-thirty," Faith said.

"Oh, boy, we'd better get going, then. We were supposed to be at Pizza Pete's at five-thirty for the planning session for Alison's shower."

"Our Thanksgiving dinner," Faith sighed. "Pizza."

"Oh, knowing Pete," Dana said, "he'll probably have turkey pizza on the menu tonight. Besides, I've always liked being unconventional. When my mother and Maggie and I lived in New York together, after my folks got divorced, we always had holiday dinners at this Chinese restaurant near our apartment. It was kind of our own crazy family tradition."

"I don't mind the pizza part," Shelley said. "I just don't understand why those girls from 407 think they should be in on the planning of Alison's shower."

"Well," Dana said, "it *was* their idea."

"Yeah," Faith said, "but Alison's our friend. She's just their housemother. We know what she likes. We're the ones who should be making these decisions."

"Well, maybe," Dana said, trying to smooth things over, "but it *was* nice of them to include us in their Thanksgiving dinner."

"Bah humbug," Faith said, and stuck out her tongue.

"Faith. Come on. That's your usual Christmas sentiment. It's only Thanksgiving now."

"All right, then," Faith said, "bah gobble gobble."

This set the three of them laughing all the way out of the locker room.

There was nobody laughing, however, at the big round table in the back of Pizza Pete's. Andy, Toby, and Jane sat in silence, stirring the ice cubes around in their diet sodas, looking grim against the cheerful murals of Venetian gondolas. It was six o'clock and the other three still hadn't shown up.

"Maybe we ought to just order without them," Toby suggested. "Maybe they got caught up in something else. They've probably got a lot to do this weekend."

"Oh, don't you see, Toby," Andy said. "They're trying to one-up us. Show us how important they are."

"Well, they *are* older," said Toby, who most of the time felt everyone was older than she was.

"They're not so much older, as too big for their britches," Jane interjected.

"Ooops," said Andy, who was seated facing the front door of the restaurant. "Speak of the devil. Or in this case . . . devils."

* * *

Dana, Faith, and Shelley waved and made their way cheerfully to the back of the restaurant, arriving at the table to find a wall of silent stares from the other three.

"Oh, boy," Shelley said breathlessly. "We're really late, I know. But we went for a swim and, well, you've heard of rapture of the deep. Well we kind of got rapture of the shallow end."

At this, Faith, Dana, and Shelley burst into laughter while Toby, Jane, and Andy just continued to stare at them.

"Oh, hey," Dana said, "we really are sorry, you know. Can we be forgiven?"

The other three exchanged silent glances, and then Jane spoke for them, in a cool, businesslike tone.

"Please. Sit down." She indicated the three vacant chairs, side by side. The seating arrangement was symbolic. The table was going to be a battlefield, one side occupied by the old girls of 407, the other side by the new girls.

"We've got a lot of planning to do," Jane went on. "First, though, we'll order the pizza."

The pizza was where the problems began.

"We'll have an extra-large mushroom and sausage," Andy told the waitress she had hailed over to the table.

"Uh," Faith said, not about to be bulldozed

by this snippy upstart. "If you don't mind, none of the three of us likes sausage. Pepperoni is *our* favorite."

Andy looked at Jane and Toby, sighed theatrically, and told the waitress in her most controlled voice, "All right. Make that one extra-large mushroom and pepperoni."

"Pepperoni and black olive," Faith said, and when Andy glared at her, she put up her hands and said, "Hey. It's our favoritest favorite. It would be a real nostalgic trip to have a good old pepperoni and black olive."

Everyone sat silently at this impasse until Toby stepped in with the suggestion, "Why don't we get two medium pizzas instead? That way everyone can get what they like."

They all nodded at the sensibleness of this, and Andy told the waitress, "Okay. Make that one medium sausage and mushroom, and one medium pepperoni and black olive for our friends here."

This compromise being made, the conversation started up again, giving Faith, who was feeling a little mischievous, the opportunity to slyly tug at the sleeve of the departing waitress and tell her in a low voice, "On their mushroom and sausage, would you add a double helping of anchovies?"

The next problem came up around Shelley's idea for a theme shower.

"It's how we always do it back in Iowa. You get a fun theme. You make it a kitchen shower.

Or a gag gift shower. Or a lingerie shower. That would be my personal recommendation . . . a lingerie shower. I'll bet Alison doesn't have a stitch of fancy lingerie."

"Shelley," Jane said, looking down at the checkered tablecloth, as if too embarrassed to look Shelley straight in the eye, "theme parties may be quite the thing where you come from out there in Idaho — "

"Iowa," Shelley corrected her.

"Yes, well, whatever," Jane said dismissively, then went on. "Anyway, here in the East, showers are occasions to give the bride lovely mementos to treasure for a lifetime, keepsakes to call back the specialness of her wedding day. Out here, we give the bride a silver tea service. We do not give her underwear."

Although she had her own ideas on the subject, Toby kept quiet. She figured Jane knew best on these matters. And so she didn't suggest the Rattlesnake Creek style of shower, which was taking the bride out to the K-Mart in Dry Gulch and buying her one of those huge boxes of dishes that have everything she'd need for her whole married life, including a gravy boat and a meat platter. And then, if the bride needed something personal, like new boots, they got them for her as a present. Toby could tell none of this would apply very well here. Alison already had plates, and probably wouldn't be needing a tough pair of cowpunching boots for living in Boston.

It was Dana who came up with a temporary solution to the dispute. "Why don't we hold off on a final gift decision until we've all had a little time to think about it. We could meet tomorrow and talk over our ideas."

The others nodded.

"All right then, tomorrow afternoon. Up in 407," Jane said, just as the pizzas arrived. Everyone dug in, pulling pieces gooey with cheese onto their plates. They were ravenous.

"Well, it's not quite turkey and trimmings," Dana said.

"This sausage has the oddest flavor," Jane said. "Rather fishy."

The third snag they hit was deciding where to have the shower.

"The Rose Garden would be nice," Jane said. "It's such a tasteful and elegant restaurant."

"It also costs an arm and a leg to eat there," Faith pointed out.

"What about right here?" Toby said. "It's my favorite restaurant."

"But Alison's not that crazy about pizza," Dana said.

"What about Mr. Rib?" Andy suggested. "It's not as good as my family's steak and rib restaurant back in Chicago, but it's the best you can do out here. And I think, given the choice of anything in the world to eat, everyone would rather have ribs."

"Are you serious?" Faith said. "Everyone would *not* rather have ribs. At least not all the time. And Alison's practically a vegetarian so she'd hardly *ever* rather have ribs."

"Faith's right," Dana said. "You're all thinking of yourselves . . . what *you* like. Try thinking of Alison . . . what she'd like. This *is* supposed to be *her* shower, after all."

"I know!" Shelley exclaimed. "Let's take her to the Holistic Café."

"That tacky *health* food restaurant?" Jane said, making the word *health* sound almost sinister.

"It's her favorite restaurant," Shelley said.

"But all those beat-up wood tables and all those macramé hangings and all that tofu. And the hippie waiters. It hardly seems like a place for a celebration."

"I could call Harvey," Faith said. "He owns the place. He's crazy about Alison. If we tell him we're making a party for her, he'll pull out all the stops."

"He'll burn incense sticks on her cake," Toby said. "That's what he did for someone's birthday at the next table, one time when I was in there."

"Well, maybe we'll have to tell him not to pull out quite *all* the stops," Faith said. "We can make sure the party is just what Alison would want."

"You know," Jane said in a bored voice, "it's getting a little tiresome listening to the three of you acting like you're the only ones who know or care about Alison."

"Yeah," Andy jumped in, eager to add her two cents' worth, "maybe you've known her longer, but who's closer to her now? Don't forget, you've been away for quite a while. Lots of things have changed with her. Why, you haven't even met David."

"Have you?" Shelley asked.

"Of course. We talked with him a little at the Leaf Rake. And we watch him on the news almost every night."

"And what do you think?" Dana asked.

"He's from Boston," Jane added, "which I take as a good sign."

"But I know Toby has her doubts," Dana said. "Don't you?"

Toby grew nervous at being prodded like this, especially by Dana, whom she wasn't sure she trusted yet.

"I think he's probably okay," she said guardedly.

"A ringing vote of confidence," Shelley teased. Toby was beginning to almost like Shelley. She was from Iowa, which wasn't that far from Texas, and she dressed in a slightly frilly way, in bright colors. Like Toby, she wasn't very stylish. The other two, Faith and Dana, were so super-chic in their designer jeans and fifties print shirts that they scared Toby a little. Of course, most of the time she even felt different from her own two roommates. Jane dressed so properly Bostonian in plain wool skirts and pants, Fair Isle sweaters, and cotton turtlenecks. And Andy was so urban cool. She even had a pair of leather disco pants.

In answer to Shelley's question about David, Toby said, "I guess he just seems a little too smooth. I like people with a few rough edges."

"Like . . ." Dana started to say. Toby thought she was going to say, "Like Randy," but instead, she said, "Like Michael."

"Yes," Toby agreed, "Michael does seem more real than David. Of course, none of us have really seen or heard how David is with Alison. Which is more important than how his hair is styled, or how he reads the news."

Everyone could agree on this point. Andy's mind, though, went further. She started to run with the idea. Toby was right. The only way they could get a true reading on David was to see how he was in private with Alison. And while she would be the first to admit that eavesdropping and spying on someone was a total invasion of their privacy, sometimes there was a more important, overriding factor. If David really was the wrong guy for Alison, didn't her friends have the duty to find out and warn her off, before it was too late!?

CHAPTER NINE

"They really ought to make every weekend four days long," Toby sighed, flopping onto her bed, stretching out the length of it, her arms above her head. She closed her eyes and contemplated this nice hunk of free time lying ahead. Here it was Thursday night and the only homework she had due Monday was her biology project — a cut-away model of the human heart. She had hollowed out four rubber balls to represent the ventricles, then pressed them up against a plexiglass sheet to hold the blood in. For the veins and arteries, she'd used clear plastic tubing. Her biggest stumbling block had been the blood. First she'd tried cherry soda, then tomato juice, then ketchup. But all of them leaked out. Finally, she hit on raspberry jello. The color was pretty close and it was staying neatly inside.

Andy thought this project was gross. She referred to it as "emergency-room art."

Jane complimented Toby on the heart's educational value, but never could seem to bring herself to look straight at it.

Toby was almost finished with it now, but she still had to make up and glue on little tags, identifying the various parts of the heart. Lying there on her bed, she had a fleeting thought about working on them tonight, before the weekend got away from her. But she waited and the thought happily passed. And never came back. Not even when Jane pulled a fresh pack of three-by-five cards from her desk drawer. "This weekend will give me a chance to write out all my French verb cards. If I work straight through tonight. . . ."

"Not tonight," Andy said. "Tonight we're all going to the Rialto."

"Why, thank you for the invitation, Andrea, but I've already seen the movie they're playing this week. *All About Eve.* It was quite excellent, actually."

"Then you won't mind seeing it again," Andy said.

"Why do I have this strange feeling, Andy, that you're trying to tell me something?"

"We're going into town?" Toby said, bewildered. "We just got back."

"Yes," Andy said, "but on the way through the lobby just now, I overheard Alison say she and David were going to see *All About Eve* tonight. If we can disguise ourselves and manage to sit in front of them in the dark, we might be able to hear what's going on between the two of them. We might be able to learn how he treats her."

"Oh, I don't know," Toby said. "Doesn't that seem a little like trespassing on their privacy?"

"Yes, of course it does," Jane said righteously.

"Come *on*!" Andy urged. "Don't you see we owe this to Alison? She's in love with this guy. Which makes her the absolute *worst* person to decide if he's okay or not. She's completely biased. For her own good, we simply have to check him out. And we can't do that if he knows we're around. He'll just put on his best face."

"You talk about him like he's Dr. Jekyll and Mr. Hyde," Jane said. "Maybe he's even more wonderful with her. Maybe he's even more smiling and sincere than when he reads the news. Maybe he doesn't have that hair spray on when they go out."

"Maybe," Andy agreed. "And maybe not. There's only one way to find out for sure. Now . . . am I going to have to do this alone, or are you two in it with me?"

A long silence descended over the room like a thick cloud. Finally Jane spoke. "Just what kind of disguises did you have in mind?"

Andy hadn't thought this far ahead, but then Toby unexpectedly said, with a slow Texas grin spreading across her freckled face, "I've got an idea."

The Rialto was Greenleaf's revival movie house. The management only ran old movies, and had fixed up the old theater so it looked a lot like it had in its heyday, the 1930's and 40's. The seats were covered in deep red velvet. Star lights twinkled in the blue ceiling. The curtain over the screen was trimmed with heavy gold fringe. There was even a big old organ off to the side of the screen, which was played when silent movies were shown. It was basically a great place, and a big favorite of Alison's.

She and David got there about ten minutes before showtime.

"You want some popcorn, sweetheart?" he asked when they'd taken off their jackets and settled into a couple of seats down near the front.

Alison nodded. "I pretty much *always* want popcorn," Alison admitted.

"I'll get an extra-super-giant-humongous-size, in that case," he said, bent over and kissed her on the forehead, then headed back up the aisle.

When he returned a few minutes later, he sat down, passed her the big cardboard bucket and a handful of paper napkins, and said,

"Wow. I just saw three of the oddest old men in the lobby."

"Odd how? How odd?" Alison asked.

"Well, maybe they're from one of those cults. They're. . . ." He turned around in his seat and quickly turned back toward the front again. "They're coming this way," he whispered.

Alison didn't dare turn to look. As it turned out, she didn't have to. In a moment, there they were . . . three old men with long gray beards and thick-lensed glasses. They were all short and bent over. And they were all dressed in black robes and red stocking caps with tassles dangling from the ends.

"*Nashca ramalomo*," one of them said to the others in some incomprehensible language, as he gestured toward the row right in front of Alison and David where three empty seats were left.

"*Dushi gra bacum*," one of the others said, nodding and tugging at the sleeves of his friends. He was, under his beard, clearly a black man. The other two, though, had dark, but more reddish complexions.

With much more foreign conversation and gesturing and backing in and out of the row, letting one, then another by in some elaborate and incomprehensible ritual of politeness, they finally got themselves seated . . . directly in front of David and Alison.

Alison was fascinated. While these little men were *so* strange, there was also something about them that was oddly familiar. She wondered if maybe she'd seen a special on their country or culture on public television.

No, not public television. Maybe at that international bazaar David had taken her to at the wharves in Boston. Those caps looked so familiar, too. It was interesting that they'd come to see an old Bette Davis movie. She wondered what they'd make of it.

"They're really *little* guys, aren't they?" David said.

"Yes," Alison agreed. "And their voices are so high-pitched for old men."

"And so loud," David added. "I hope they're not going to rattle on like that once the movie starts."

They didn't. They settled in and watched like everyone else. Alison almost forgot they were there until one time she thought she heard one of them asking for the M&Ms. But that couldn't be. Or maybe he'd said *emo nems*, or something else from their language.

But then, a ways into the movie, when Bette Davis headed into a party she was throwing and said, "Fasten your seatbelts, everybody. It's going to be a bumpy ride," one of the little men said what distinctly sounded to Alison like, "All *right*, girl!" And he said it in a voice that sounded like someone not from a foreign country, but from Chicago, Illinois. Andy Cord.

Click. From there everything fell into place in Alison's mind. The beards and caps were from Canby Hall's production two years ago of *Santa's Workshop*. The gowns belonged to the Canby Hall Chorale. She smiled to herself in the dark before cupping her hand over David's ear and whispering very low, "Our little men are really three of my girls, I'm afraid."

He turned to her and gave her a "what's up?" look.

"I'm not sure. Maybe they want to check you out. Make sure you're a suitable suitor for me."

He nodded, then grinned, and whispered, "Want to have a little fun with them?"

"Oh, yes!" she said, and squeezed his hand. He waited a minute and then began commenting on the movie in a voice just loud enough to be heard as far as the row in front of them.

"Boy, Lissy," he said, making up the dumbest nickname for her that he could think of on the spur of the moment, "I sure don't get why these women want to be famous actresses when they could be staying home, cleaning up the house, and making dinner for their husbands. That's the only real satisfaction in life for women, making their men happy."

"Oh, I know, Davey. But do you think I'll be able to make you a good enough wife?"

"That depends. As I told you, I'm very demanding, but I'm making a detailed list, which I'll give you on our wedding day. Then you'll know how much starch I like in my shirts, how many minutes I like my eggs boiled, and which drugstore sells the special Italian toothpaste I like. It'll be a full-time job keeping me happy, but if you work very hard, I'm sure there'll be a pat on the head for my little wifey when I get home at night."

"But will you help me at all around the house?" she asked in a sugary voice the girls had never heard her use around the dorm.

"Of course not," David said sternly. "Housework is boring for men. We must be free to devote ourselves to our important careers. In a marriage, someone has to make sacrifices . . . and it's the wife."

"I guess you're right," Alison said, sounding like she was being persuaded to his point of view.

Andy and Jane could hardly stand this. Toby leaned over toward them and said in a low voice, "He sounds worse than a cowboy."

"He's impossible. He sounds like he's from medieval times. Or one of those countries where the women have to walk so many paces behind their husbands. Or pull the ox carts."

"It's worse than our worst fears," Jane admitted.

They all pressed against their seat backs and slunk down in hopes of hearing more.

And Alison and David were only too ready to give them more.

"Well, Lissy, my mother ought to be able to answer any questions you might have about management of the household."

"You mean I can ask her at the wedding?"

"Or anytime after. I did tell you, didn't I, that I've asked her to move in with us?"

"I guess you must've forgot to mention it," Alison muttered.

"She'll be a big help to you with the mush-rooms," he said.

"Mushrooms?"

"Well, you wouldn't want to be home all day with nothing to do, would you? After you finish with the cooking and cleaning and laundry, there ought to still be more than enough time left over to raise a nice little mushroom crop in the basement. Then you and mother can take them to the outdoor markets and sell them. She'll be good company for you."

"But I'll have my own friends for com-pany," Alison protested meekly. "And I ex-pect I'll get visits from some of my favorite girls from Canby Hall."

"I'm not so sure that would be a good idea," David said sternly. "They might put notions in that pretty little head of yours. Especially that bunch from 407. Didn't you say that Andy Cord wants to be a ballet dancer? And that Jane Barrett has hopes of being a writer? And that October Houston wants to run a cattle ranch of her own? Ridiculous! Those girls will never do any of those things. If they're lucky, they'll graduate and find nice young men who'll marry them and let them darn their socks."

"We will not!!" Andy shouted. The girls turned around in their seats, fuming, forgetting that they were in disguise, forgetting even that they were in a theater.

"Sssssshhh," said about thirty people in the audience. Which made the girls turn back and slide down in their seats in embarrassment.

David and Alison leaned forward at this moment, until their faces were right behind the girls' heads, and said in low voices, "Gotcha!"

This made all three girls grin sheepishly under their beards. They got up and slunk out and went into the ladies' room, where they took off their caps and robes and pulled off their glued-on beards. Andy helped Jane and Toby cold cream their red makeup away. By the time the three of them emerged, the movie was just over and David and Alison were coming up the aisle into the lobby. They both started smiling as soon as they saw the roommates. All three girls thought David looked even cuter in person than when he was all fixed up on tv. He was wearing glasses for the movie, and just an old gray sweat shirt and a pair of unironed khakis.

"You figured us out right away, didn't you?" Jane asked Alison bashfully.

"Well, I'm getting pretty good at this," Alison said. "The other night Dana, Faith, and Shelley turned up at my door hiding inside mudpacks to surprise me. Now you three are impersonating foreign dignitaries so you can spy on me. Why am I being tormented like this?" She threw the back of her hand up to her forehead in a gesture of woe, but she was smiling as she did it.

"We just love you, Alison," Andy said. "We had to check this guy out. Make sure he's good enough for you." Then she turned to David and said, "You really had us going there."

"You didn't mean *any* of the things you said, did you?" asked Toby, who wanted to make absolutely sure David had only been kidding.

"Not a word," he said. "Actually, it was hard for me to think up enough awful stuff to pull the joke off."

"You should've just asked me," Alison told the girls, as they all walked out through the darkened lobby together. "I would've given you the full rundown on David's wonderfulness."

"But people in love are the worst judges of character," Andy protested.

"But Andrea," David said, "you know Alison well enough to know that she could never fall in love in the first place with anyone who was a jerk. Actually, before we decided to get married — well, that is, before Alison proposed and I accepted — she grilled me pretty thoroughly on my attitudes. We made a commitment to a marriage that would be a partnership of equals. That means equal chances for success in all ways. For instance, Alison would like to get a graduate degree in art history and I'll support us both while she does. But then I get to take some time off to just loaf and fool around with my painting, while she works as a curator or professor."

"And if we decide to have kids," Alison said, "I take off the first year with the baby, and David plays househusband for the second year."

The three roommates took in all this information. By now they were all standing out on Main Street, where the night was crispy cold. They buttoned and zipped up their jackets and pulled on their gloves, and were about to say good-night when David offered to buy everybody hot chocolate at the Tutti Frutti ice-cream parlor up the street.

"Great!" all three roommates answered. They were convinced now that David was great and that Alison loved him for great reasons. Each of them was, in fact, secretly thinking that David was just the kind of guy she herself might marry when the time came.

Halfway down the block, Toby came up and tugged on David's sleeve and asked him the final question that was hanging around in her mind, bothering her just a little.

"You don't *really* call Alison 'Lissy,' do you?"

"I wouldn't dare," David said. "She'd probably bite me."

"And you'd better watch out," Alison said, grabbing onto his arm. "I haven't had my rabies shot this year."

CHAPTER TEN

Jane came tearing into 407, a little out of breath from running all the way up from the pay phones.

"He said he'd *love* to come to the wedding with me!" she told Toby and Andy, who were just barely awake. Jane had gotten up early to call Neal in Boston, before he went out to the harbor with his father. She knew this was the day they were pulling the family sailboat out of the water for the winter.

"Mmrphmmrph," Toby said, which might mean anything. She was hard to translate when she first woke up. Nearly everything she said then sounded like *mmrphmmrph*. She was the World's Soundest Sleeper. At night she burrowed into her pillow and dropped off in about ten seconds, then immediately began a soft snoring that lasted until she got up the next morning. When she lifted her head from the pillow eight hours later, her eyes were usually stuck shut, her red curly hair smashed against one side of her head or the other, depending on which way she'd slept through the night.

"Boy, I hope I never get invited to a come-as-you-are breakfast," she said once, seeing how scrunched up she looked before she'd had a shower and breakfast.

"So who cares about Mr. Rebel, Cary Slade, anyway?" Jane went on, twirling around the room. Andy was sitting up in bed now. Toby was trying to get her eyes open and focused on Jane, who was moving way too fast for her. But Jane went on, oblivious to the fact that her audience wasn't quite ready for her. "So phooey on conceited Cary Slade. I have a date for the wedding now with Cornelius Worthington the Third. My Neal. And he's positively *thrilled* to be coming. He said it would give him an opportunity to waltz with me."

"Waltz?" said Andy, who was into almost all kinds of dancing, from disco to her main love, ballet, but had never in her life waltzed.

"Oh, Neal is a fabulous ballroom dancer. He took lessons. You know, to be ready for all the debutante parties he'll be going to."

"What's a debutante party?" Toby asked, sitting up blearily.

"Oh, Toby." Jane moaned at how hopelessly unsocialized her roommate was. Then she instantly felt bad for letting her exasperation show. To smooth things over, she said,

"Hey. Why don't you come down to breakfast with me? Now that I've got my social life straightened out and am no longer a bundle of nerve endings, I'm suddenly starved."

Andy decided to come along, too, but by then they had no time to spare. The three of them ran down the stairs and across campus to the dining hall, making it just minutes before breakfast hours ended and the doors to the hall were closed.

The campus dining hall was a beautiful room, with one long wall made up entirely of windows facing onto a meadow, which was now turning shades of rust and gold. At lunch and dinner, the hall was packed, a battle-ground of a hundred conversations. But at breakfast, it was nearly empty, and so a much quieter, nicer place to be. The food was better then, too.

"It's hard to ruin an egg and a piece of toast," was how Andy put it. Being from a restaurant family, she lived in a constant state of amazement at the food served at Canby Hall.

This morning the three of them went through the line and took doughnuts from Maggie's roommate, Dee. She ran the dough-nut machine and always set aside a few chocolate-covered ones for the girls from 407.

The main dish today was billed as "eggs Benny."

"Uh, excuse me," Andy said to Mrs. Sharp,

the head dietician, who was passing by on the other side of the steam tables. "Could you tell me what exactly is in eggs Benny?"

"You heard of eggs Benedict?" Mrs. Sharp asked gruffly.

Andy nodded and said, "Yes. Poached eggs on English muffins with Canadian bacon underneath and hollandaise sauce on top."

"Well, eggs Benny's sort of like that."

On this recommendation, the girls all took plates of eggs Benny and found a table. When they inspected this dish more closely, they discovered that "sort of" like eggs Benedict meant that the eggs were scrambled from powdered mix, the muffin was a piece of dry toast, the ham was bologna and the hollandaise was melted processed cheeselike food product.

"Not too bad," Toby said, when she'd swallowed a mouthful.

"You've been here too long," Andy said, but she was eating hers, too. They all decided that eggs Benny fell into one of the better categories of Canby Hall food — gross but tasty.

"So what are you two wearing to this shower tonight?" Toby asked the others, not trusting her judgment on these high-level social matters.

"Well, since they steamrolled us into having it at that hippie hangout," Jane said, "I'm thinking of wearing bell-bottomed jeans and reflector aviator sunglasses."

"Oh, it'll be okay," Toby said. "They talked that guy Harvey out of the carob-wheat germ cake and insisted he make something chocolate. We'll bring the music — all Alison's favorite stuff on tape. And we'll be bringing her our presents. So it's really going to be *our* party. So don't worry. It'll go just fine."

"I hope so," Jane said huffily. "As for what to wear, I don't know what to tell you. Your best casual outfit, I'd say. I, for instance, am going to wear my blue cashmere V neck, a pink oxford cloth shirt, and my navy narrow-wale corduroy skirt."

"Hmmm," Toby said, thinking, "maybe I'll go over to my extra locker and pull out my dress boots with the snakeskin inserts."

"I've never seen those boots," Andy said.

"What extra locker?" Jane asked. "I thought everyone here got *one* locker."

"If you got even one, you're lucky," Andy said. "I still haven't been able to *find* mine. It's 986 and I've never seen any lockers anywhere higher than 800."

"Someone else told me they've got one of those mystery lockers," Toby said. "Well, you should take my extra one. I don't know how I got it. A computer blip, I guess."

Just then, Patrice Allardyce came through the dining hall with a gaunt, tall young woman. The girls knew she was probably another candidate for Alison's job.

As they passed by, they heard the candidate

say, "Oh, this food looks much too lavish. If I get the job, I'll press for a no-frills regimen here. Porridge in the mornings, for instance. It's been a staple of boarding school life since Victorian times. Of course, there could be treats on holidays, and kippers every Sunday."

"Kippers!?" Andy, Toby, and Jane said nearly simultaneously, and crossed their eyes at each other as the candidate passed.

When Toby got to Main after breakfast, the halls were dimly lit and eerily empty. And so she was surprised, on turning the corner into the corridor where her lockers were, to see a girl with long dark hair hunkering down in front of one, turning the dial on the combination lock.

When Toby got closer, she saw that it was Dana. And when Dana saw Toby, she jumped up, startled.

"They've changed my combination," she said in a sad voice, and pulled a dusty pink band off her head. She was wearing gray sweats and pale blue leg warmers. It looked like she'd been running.

"I think they probably switch the locks around every year," Toby said, just trying to be helpful.

"Kind of symbolic, don't you think?" Dana said.

Toby shook her head to show she didn't understand.

"Well, the thing is, I can come back, like I am this weekend. But I'm not *really* back. I'm just a visitor. They've changed my lock, and I don't know who the new teachers are, or what the latest gossip is, or what play the drama department is putting on this term. Almost all my old friends are gone, and the ones I can find have, well, changed. I'm not even sure they're my friends anymore."

Toby nodded. Now she was beginning to get it. "You mean Randy, don't you?"

"Maybe. You know about us, don't you?"

"A little," Toby admitted. "You used to go together."

"That was a million years ago. But when I ran into him, he acted like it had all happened just yesterday, like we could just pick up where we'd left off before. And then he was hurt when I didn't jump at this idea. I just don't understand him. I was only trying to be friendly. And now he's furious at me. He rode off at about a hundred miles an hour. That was always one of the darndest things about him. He's always on a horse, so he can always storm off in a dramatic way, leaving you in a cloud of dust."

Toby processed all this. She tried to picture what had gone on between Randy and Dana that had so upset them both. At first imagining an emotionally charged scene between the two of them just made her jealous. But then she started thinking about things from Randy's point of view and felt bad for him, still carrying a torch for someone who'd left long ago.

"Maybe he misunderstood your coming out to see him," she told Dana, as she went to open her own locker. As soon as she said this, she was sorry. While she wanted to defend Randy, she wasn't very comfortable talking about him, especially with Dana, whose motives she still wasn't quite sure she could trust.

"Misunderstood what?" Dana asked. "He couldn't have thought anything was really going to happen between us again."

Toby reached way back in the locker and pulled out the packet of newspaper wrapped around and around with twine that held her special boots.

Finally she said, "A couple of years ago I was in a horse race. It was a Future Ranchers Day out at the county fairgrounds. I didn't have the chance of a snowball in a heat wave. At least half the riders were older and better than I was, and Max, though I love him dearly, well, he's a pretty old guy in horse years. But I wanted to win so much that I just kind of forgot all the reasons I was not *going* to win."

"And you wound up coming in first," guessed Dana, who had seen all the movies of underdogs winning in the end.

"Nope. Came in dead last," Toby said. "And then I was furious. Went around in a blazing rage all day. They should've used a fire extinguisher on me."

"Are you saying Randy wanted something to happen between us, and so he didn't let himself see that it wasn't going to?" Dana asked.

"Maybe the whole thing isn't as over for him as it is for you."

"Oh," Dana said, and then grew quiet for a moment. Then she asked Toby, "How do you know him so well? How do you know what's going on in his mind?"

"We're friends," Toby said, but didn't offer any more. This was closest to the truth, even if it wasn't exactly what Toby wanted. She'd like to go from being friends to something more. And maybe that would happen someday. Unless, of course, Dana Morrison, in spite of all her protestations of not being interested in Randy anymore, swooped him up and away. Toby made herself stop this line of thinking. It only made her nervous.

She would have been twice as nervous if she could have read Dana's mind at the moment. She would have seen Dana reconsidering Randy. His impulsiveness in the woods, his mysterious connection with Toby, made him seem less like the guy she'd left behind and more like a person of unpredictable moods and enticing secrets.

She wasn't sure exactly what she was feeling

. . . but something, that was for sure. Maybe the old spark between her and Randy was reigniting. Maybe something would happen this weekend that could continue after she got back East in the spring.

She didn't voice any of these thoughts to Toby. They were way too unformed and probably dumb. She'd be embarrassed to talk about them to anyone. Instead, she watched Toby unwrap, in the dim glow of the corridor lights, the most beautiful pair of cowboy boots she'd ever seen.

"Wow," Dana said, and whistled low.

Toby looked up and grinned. "They *are* great, aren't they? I'm going to wear them to the shower tonight."

"Show everyone what Texas cool looks like, eh?" Dana said. She liked Toby, and thought that if they'd been at Canby Hall together, they might have been good friends. "Alison told us you guys gave her and David a hard time last night."

Toby grinned again.

"Alison's supposed to introduce us to him this morning. They're having us for brunch. We still haven't really met him, you know," Dana said. "I suppose my doubts will disappear when I get to know him."

"You've never seen two people happier together," Toby assured her.

"On the other hand, I don't think I've ever

seen anyone as miserable as Michael last night. He was walking across the campus, practically bumped into us on one of the paths, and didn't even see us. And he used to be our friend."

"If you used to be friends," Toby said, "maybe one of you should go see him, try to help him out."

"I know. I've been thinking about that. But I'm the wrong one to go. I'm too nervous. Before, he was always the wise one, the one with the answers and the Kleenex ready for me to cry into. I don't think I could handle a complete reversal of roles. I mean, what would I do if he actually *did* start weeping or something? What would I do if he fell apart on me? Maybe Faith should be the one to go see him. She's always cool and collected."

Dana stopped for a moment, then looked seriously at Toby and said, "I know you guys all like David, but what I really want is that Alison would just let him get into his little green car and go back to Boston. And then I want her to get back together with Michael." Dana lifted her wrist to the light and looked at the face of the huge thirties-style man's watch her mother had given her for graduation.

"Oh, my!" she exclaimed, more to herself than to Toby. "Alison's brunch! I was supposed to be up there fifteen minutes ago."

She started running down the hall, but stopped when she got to the end, and turned to say to Toby, "You'll outdo us all in those boots tonight, you know."

And then she was gone.

CHAPTER ELEVEN

Faith was also in a rush to get to Alison's brunch. She had been in town, taking photos of the village green in the early morning mist. These were for a class photo essay on "Disappearing New England" . . . places in this part of the country that had remained untouched by the modern world.

She was having a good time taking pictures of old, familiar landmarks around Greenleaf. The white frame, steepled Presbyterian Church. The old weatherbeaten barn out at the Dillards' farm, with its nearly worn-away signs for Mail Pouch chewing tobacco and John Deere tractors. The old cement watering trough in front of the town hall.

Unlike Dana, Faith was totally enjoying her visit. She wasn't tormented by unresolved feelings about being back here. She loved Canby Hall, but was also really happy in her freshman year at Rochester. And she wasn't tormented by worries about what to do with her old Greenleaf boyfriend, because she was still going with him. Only now Johnny Bates wasn't entirely a Greenleaf boy anymore, because he was in *his* freshman year at Michigan State, in the police administration program there.

Faith still hated that Johnny wanted to be a cop and risk the same fate that had befallen her father, a policeman killed in the line of duty. But she loved Johnny in spite of this career decision. She wished he were here now, but Michigan was too far for him to come home for Thanksgiving. They'd have to wait until Christmas to get together.

For now, she was just happy to have a four-day break from classes and homework, to take pictures, and enjoy her friends, and think uncomplicated thoughts. She wasn't even troubled about Alison marrying David. She figured that was Alison's business, nothing to get all riled up about.

Actually she wasn't riled up about anything. Well, except for one minor annoyance. Andy Cord. Faith still couldn't quite shake Andy's remark about Faith's lack of true black spirit. Was it possible that there was some truth to this? She *had* been living in an essentially white world for a while now. Maybe she *was* losing some of her black identity, and some of her feeling of closeness to other blacks. Every time she thought about this, it made her uncomfortable, and then annoyed with Andy for having planted this seed of self-doubt in her mind.

Then, as Faith was running toward Baker, her braid bands clinking, her camera and lenses dangling from her shoulders, suddenly there she was . . . Andy. She was coming across the lawn in a raspberry-colored sweat shirt and pants and a purple down vest, a small duffel bag thrown over one shoulder. It was kind of weird — as if Faith's thinking about her had conjured her up, like a magician pulling a rabbit from a hat.

It was an awkward situation on both sides. They couldn't really snub each other. They had to be at least civil until the wedding was over. Neither wanted their petty conflict to spoil anything for Alison. On the other hand, neither wanted to lose points by being really nice to the other. And so the conversation was like a plant with lots of tiny, hidden thorns.

"Hello, Andrea," Faith said, when they had gotten so close they had to say *something*. "On your way to practice your *ballet*?" She said the word *ballet* in a slightly amused tone, as if she were noting Andy's interest in championship tiddlywinks, or her popsicle stick collection.

"Yes," Andy said haughtily. "The dance studio should be empty this morning. You off to take some of your little snapshots?" she asked, figuring two could play this game.

"Nope," Faith said, now acknowledging the dig. "I'm on my way back. Now I'm off to the brunch Alison's having for me and Shelley and Dana. David will be there, too. He's apparently dying to meet us."

"How nice that Alison's having a private little brunch just for you. I hope all you old, dear friends have tons of fun."

"I'll try," Faith said. "But if any of those nasty white folks are mean to me, I'll rush right down to cry on your shoulder. You've been such a sister to me ever since we've met." To cap off the remark, she gave Andy a fake "old pals" punch on the arm, and then turned and walked off, leaving Andy standing in the middle of the path, fuming.

Faith and Dana . . . and Shelley (who had slept in this morning, barely waking in time) were on their various ways to the brunch up in The Penthouse. Coffee was brewing there, along with trouble between Alison and David.

Actually, the trouble was *over* the coffee. David had made it very strong, the way he liked it. When Alison poured herself a cup and took a sip, she ran straight to the sink and spit it out. David watched this in astonishment. Alison turned back toward him, wiped her mouth with a handy dish towel, and forced a smile through her embarrassment.

"A little strong, isn't it?" she said.

"It's how I always make it," he said.

"Who do you usually make it for, long-haul truck drivers?"

She was only kidding, but he took it the wrong way. David considered himself a great cook, and he took this as a slur on his culinary capabilities. He retaliated by saying, "Well, I do like something a little stronger than that dishwater *you* call coffee."

Now it was Alison's turn to take offense. She was not very experienced in the kitchen, and was really nervous about putting this brunch together. Usually, when she had friends over, her basic kitchen equipment was her index finger and her telephone. That is, she phoned to get a pizza delivered. And so she felt David was trying to pull her already shaky confidence out from underneath her.

"You're trying to make me more nervous than I already am," she accused him.

"Who's trying to make *whom* nervous?" he retorted. "You're the one who's putting *me* on display here for inspection by your friends. But seeing as I'm not even appreciated, why should I bother to go through this at all?"

"Darling," Alison pleaded.

"Don't 'darling' me. Every day I have to meet someone new in your life and smile and talk nice and pass inspection. Last week it was five cups of tea and a police-level interrogation from your great aunt Hildegarde. Today it's the old girls from the dorm. Well, I'm tired of it. So if you'll excuse me, I think I'll just skip this morning's little gathering."

"But . . ." Alison started to say.

"But what?" David countered, now flushed with anger. "They're your friends. You can entertain them."

"But where are you going?"

He glared at her for a second before saying, "I'm not sure. Someplace where there isn't any chance of hearing about weddings."

He looked at Alison to see her reaction, but she was looking over his shoulder, past him, toward the door. He turned around to see what Alison was looking at. There in the doorway, their mouths open, their eyes large with dismay, were Dana, Faith, and Shelley.

CHAPTER TWELVE

Angry and embarrassed and flustered, David stormed away from Alison, past the girls, out the door, and down the hall. They were all still for a moment. Alison stood in the middle of her small kitchen as if she were rooted to the worn linoleum floor. Tears streamed silently down her cheeks.

The three girls came softly into the room and tried in their own ways to take care of their old housemother. Faith took from Alison's hand the spatula she was holding, then turned off the burner under the iron frying pan full of now-burnt eggs.

Shelley added hot water to the coffee to dilute it. She poured cups for all of them, then brought the coffee and a plate full of sweet rolls into the living room.

Dana put an arm over Alison's shoulder and led her over to the old couch.

The three old roommates gathered around

and sat silently waiting, giving Alison a little while to pull herself together. When she had finally dried her eyes and seemed ready to talk, Faith offered a possible explanation for what had just happened.

"That guy's got the pre-wedding jitters. That's all that's going on. It's plain and clear."

"You think so?" Alison said with hope in her voice.

Faith nodded vigorously. "You should've seen my cousin Roxanne the day before her wedding. She and Frederick had such a fight that he drove all the way to Georgia, and spent the night before the wedding in some small town, and didn't tell anybody where he was."

Alison's eyes opened with interest. "What did your cousin do?"

Faith chuckled. "Oh, Roxanne's a strong-minded woman. She just got her hair done, and put her dress on, and had her father drive her over to the church. When the clock struck ten, she nodded to that organist to start up that wedding march, and she headed right on down that aisle."

"Alone?" Alison said, incredulous. "Without the groom waiting at the altar!?"

"Well, he wasn't in sight when she started down the aisle, but he managed to get himself there by the time she reached the altar."

"But how could she count on him? She

could've been embarrassed for the rest of her life."

"Not Roxanne. I told you she was a strong woman. She knew that *he* knew that if he didn't show, she'd make him miserable for the rest of his days. And so, at the last minute, he got some sense into his head and managed to get back to town and put on his blue suit and scoot over to that church and marry her."

"How did it all work out?" Alison asked.

"Well, they've been married five years now and they're still the love birds. They've got a darling little boy, too."

"And Frederick's happy?"

"Of course he's happy," Faith said. "He wasn't ever really *un*happy. He just had the jitters. Jitters aren't really real. It's like how heat lightning doesn't have anything to do with rain. It's just loose static on the air."

Faith sounded so positive, that Alison was briefly reassured. That is, until she noticed that Faith was the only one saying anything. Dana and Shelley were sipping their coffee and keeping quiet in a way that was beginning to seem ominous.

"Come on," she urged them, "talk to me. Speak now or, as they say, forever hold your peace."

"Well . . ." Dana began, then went silent again.

"Well, what?" Alison encouraged her.

"Well, does it seem even the tiniest bit

possible that you and David are moving a little fast? I mean, how long have you known each other . . . a few weeks?"

"No. Let's see," Alison said, looking off into space, then down at her fingers as she counted backward. "November. October. September. August. July. June. May. Nearly seven months."

"Alison!" Dana gasped. "*We* were still here in May. And we had no idea."

"Well, I *knew* him, but I wasn't going with him. I guess I was too nervous to risk telling anyone. I was still with Michael and . . . well, you see."

"If you were still going with Michael, how did you even *meet* David?" Shelley chimed in.

Alison grinned sheepishly.

"Actually, I met him at a party I went to with Michael. In Boston. David was there . . . with a date. I recognized him from the tv, and thought he was probably a stuck-on-himself celebrity. And so I deliberately didn't talk to him the whole evening. I guess he took that for playing hard to get. Anyway, he came over and told me he'd been admiring me from afar all night, or some malarkey like that. And then Michael was there, *very* there, if you know what I mean, helping me into my coat, and off we went. I didn't give David another thought until the next week when he called me."

"To say he was admiring you from even farther afar?" Faith said.

Alison laughed.

"No, as I remember, it was about a special segment he was going to be doing on his news show. Something about trends in learning. He was trying to talk to people involved in various areas of education, and could he interview me briefly? Well, who could say no to that? It seemed so innocent."

"Yeah, yeah," Dana said, giving Alison a sly wink and an elbow in the ribs.

"I'll admit I probably should've been suspicious when he suggested holding the interview at Roberto's restaurant. All that red velvet and low lights and those strolling violinists."

"Strolling violinists!" Shelley exclaimed.

"They help give any interview that professoinal atmosphere," Faith deadpanned.

"All right, you guys. Stop. I know I was a little naive. But by the time I got the picture that David didn't just want to interview me, I didn't just want to be interviewed. We had so much to talk about, right from the start. It was like we'd known each other all our lives. We really are soulmates, I think."

Dana, Faith, and Shelley didn't know what to say to this.

Alison looked into the blank wall of their eyes and said, defensively, "Oh, I know it doesn't look like it from what you saw today, but really, he's not like that usually. I think Faith is probably right. The poor guy's been through a real mill of my relatives and friends. He has to perform every day for his work, and then come home and perform for all these new people I'm introducing him to. I think he's just totally stressed out. I think we both are. Last week, I was the one who blew up. Over the something his uncle sent us for a wedding gift."

"What kind of something?" Shelley asked.

"Well, that's just it. It's definitely something, but you can't come up with a more precise definition than that. It's ceramic, kind of an urn. But it also has a handle on top. It's painted with green and black blobs, kind of like camouflage. You can see the problem I was having coming up with a thank-you note. 'Dear Uncle George, Thank you so much for the lovely. . . .' But David thought I could finesse it somehow. I told him why didn't *he* write the note, and when he didn't leap right to it, I threw the something at the wall."

"You didn't," Dana said.

"I did," Alison said.

"Wow," Dana said in a very quiet voice, "I can't imagine you and Michael ever having a fight like that."

"Oh," Alison said, "so that's it. You think I've betrayed Michael, thrown him over for a gorgeous blond television personality. That I've temporarily lost my usual good sense."

"Well?" Dana asked. "Have you?"

Alison sighed and sank into the squooshy back cushions of the old sofa. She pushed her ever-sliding glasses back up on her nose and said, "I don't know. I really don't. By the time David came along, things were already winding down with Michael. More and more we were talking about the school, or problems the girls were having. And then one night when we were up at his house, sitting in the living room with the French doors open, the summer night breezes wafting through the room, Beethoven on the stereo, he turned to me and said, 'Alison, do you know that the SAT scores of Canby Hall girls went down four points this year?'

"Well, I think that was the moment when I could actually hear the hissing of the romance going out of our relationship."

"But don't all relationships kind of — well, simmer down after a while?" Shelley asked. "I've been going with Paul off and on for several years now, and I can't exactly say my heart goes boom-boom anymore just because he walks into a room. But what I feel for him runs deeper now than it ever did. I guess what I'm asking is . . . well, you don't think you're just going for the excitement, do you? Because David is bound to seem more exciting right now than old-shoe Michael. But what about in six months? What about after you find out that David has his less than glamorous side?

That he leaves his dirty laundry in a pile in the corner of the bathroom? That he forgets to put the cap back on the soda bottle when he puts it back in the refrigerator, so that it loses all its fizz? Then what?"

Everyone, even Alison, had to laugh at the absurdity of Shelley's examples in the midst of this serious discussion.

"Oh, you three are so good for me," Alison said. "And I really appreciate your concern. And I don't know, maybe I'm making the biggest mistake in my life. I'll tell you, there's nothing like the tension of a wedding to get a person so rattled she doesn't know right from left. But all the plans are set now and I'm not one to go back on a decision once I've made it. And so, for better or worse, it looks like I'm going to marry David Gordon on Saturday."

There was a pause here while everyone sat there not knowing what to say. Clearly Alison did not want to discuss things further at the moment. Finally she broke the dead silence by jumping up and beckoning to the others. "Now come into the kitchen with me and let's give this brunch a second chance!"

She said this with hearty cheerfulness, but Dana was sure she could hear a hollowness underneath. Shelley, meanwhile, was worrying that she and Dana had put doubts about David into Alison's head, and now she wondered if they'd done the right thing. Faith, on the other hand, after having been so calm and collected about him, was wondering if she should have joined in warning Alison off this mariage. All in all, the four of them were in such a muddle that they steered away from the subject of marriage and weddings and showers and brides and grooms for the rest of the meal.

Instead, they got busy in the kitchen and burnt another pan of eggs and scorched the toast and made a pot of coffee that was way too weak this time. This comedy of errors put them all in a better mood, and they began reminiscing, laughing, and talking about their days at Canby Hall. They talked about some serious things. . . . Shelley's desperate homesickness when she first arrived. The mean tricks played on them by their archenemy, Pamela Young, the time she decided to break up the friendship of the girls in 407. The broken heart Dana had suffered over Bret Harper, the best-looking guy to ever appear at Oakley Prep. Where was he now? they all wondered.

Mostly, though, they remembered the stupid, silly things. How embarrassed Faith had been when Sheff Adams, her heartthrob of the moment, had caught her at a midnight fire drill outside in her ultrascuzzy robe. The millions of pranks and jokes they'd played on each other, on Alison, on Patrice Allardyce. Which brought them to all the times Alison had smoothed things over with Ms. Allardyce for them. And all the other times she'd been there to bail them out of trouble.

They also remembered how many times they'd come, together and individually, to this very apartment, to cry on the shoulder that was always there, to mutter secrets and problems into the ear that was always ready to listen. All three of them loved Alison and, underneath their laughter and banter, were worried about her right now.

It was Dana who first glanced at her watch and saw that it was getting late. They still had a lot to do before Alison's shower. She told Shelley and Faith that they'd better get going.

"We've got a shower to put together, you know," she told Alison.

"But if you think the marriage is a big mistake, maybe you don't want to have the shower anymore," Alison replied.

"Alison," Faith said as she picked up a few dishes and headed toward the kitchen with them, "this shower's for you. It's about our loving you and wanting you to be happy. As for *how* you're going to be happy, and *who* you ought to marry, or even *if* you ought to get married, well — that's for you to figure out. But we'll be behind you no matter what you decide."

"And we'd throw this little party for you even if you weren't getting married," Shelley offered.

"We'd just get Toby to round up horses for all of us and ride out in the sunset. And instead of a bridal shower it would be a *bridle* shower," Dana said.

"Or instead of a whole dinner, we could just eat peanut candy," Faith said as the three of them headed for the door. When everyone gave her blank looks, she grinned and explained, "That way it would be a *brittle* shower."

Alison groaned and covered her ears against the puns as she pushed the girls out the door and on their way.

CHAPTER THIRTEEN

Faith, Shelley, and Dana headed straight down from The Penthouse to 407. Andy, Toby, and Jane were there waiting for them, as planned, to get together and decide on a present for Alison.

Dana could sense tension form in the room as they entered, like steam condensing in cold air. The younger girls were flopped on their beds, talking animatedly with each other. But when they saw the old roommates at the door, they fell into complete silence.

"Please," Jane said formally, "sit down."

Dana and Faith pulled up desk chairs. Shelley just dropped to the floor and sat with her legs crossed yoga-style.

This is going to be worse than the pizza dinner, Dana thought. She looked over and smiled at Toby, the only possible friend it seemed she had among these three. Which was weird, really, because Toby, protective or jealous over Randy, was the one with the most cause to dislike Dana. Instead, she seemed fair and open-minded. Not the other two, though. Jane was so frosty, especially toward Shelley, whom she clearly considered a hopeless hick from the boondocks. Even worse was how hostile Andy was toward Faith. And Dana could tell that Faith and Shelley, in return, felt very much on the defensive. All in all, it seemed unlikely that this group would ever mesh and become friends. Best to scale down goals, Dana thought, and just focus on getting this shower put together. She took the lead in the discussion.

"I suppose the first thing we ought to figure out is how much we've got to spend. Then we can go from there onto deciding what to buy."

"Uh, well, we sort of have a plan," Andy said, edgily, as if expecting this plan, whatever it was, to get squelched by the older girls.

Toby, though, didn't seem at all flustered, just enthusiastic.

"We were just talking about it before you got here," she said. "It was Jane's great idea, really."

The three older girls all turned to Jane, who grew shy under this sudden attention. Nervously, she tossed her long blond hair back over the shoulder of her mint-green turtleneck. She sat up on her bed and cleared her throat and then hesitantly expressed her idea.

"It's probably not all that great an idea. I was just telling Andy and Toby about the traditional rhyme for brides:

> *Something old,*
> *Something new,*
> *Something borrowed,*
> *Something blue.*

And we came up with this idea that instead of getting Alison one big gift, we get her four smaller presents that fit the different parts of the poem."

"We figured we could draw lots for who gets her what," Andy said excitedly.

At first, hearing this, Faith wanted to deflate Andy's fun, say something snide about the plan. But in her heart of hearts she had to admit it *was* a pretty good idea. And it was something Alison would really like. Also, looking over at Dana and Shelley, she could see they were already into the spirit of it. And so she put away her sarcasm and listened as Toby spelled out the details.

"We figured that since there are four categories and six of us, we'd make two slips for each category and then all draw. If two of us pick the same one, we go shopping for that present together."

As soon as Toby said this, Faith knew she was going to get paired up with Andy. It was one of those little twists of fate she could always see coming from a mile off. And so when they'd all taken their turns pulling slips of paper out of Toby's Stetson cowboy hat and opening them up, and Faith saw that she'd drawn "something new," she was certain that Andy had, too.

"Anybody got 'something blue'?" Shelley asked. No one had, so she was off on her own. So was Toby with "something borrowed." Jane and Dana had both drawn "something old" and were already planning which junk and antique shops in Greenleaf to hit, as Faith handed her slip to Andy.

"Looks like we're a pair," she said, laying as much sarcasm on the statement as she could.

"Yeah, I'm thrilled, too," Andy said. "You want to draw another slip?"

"No," Faith said, "it'll be okay. We can just run over to the mall and pick something up real fast." Then under her breath she added, "If we keep it down to an hour or so, we can probably keep from murdering each other, don't you think?"

"I'll bring a straitjacket in case you start looking homicidal," Andy said, also in a low voice. The others didn't hear. Everyone was preoccupied with their own mission.

"Everybody meet back here at four!" Jane shouted, as they broke off from one another on the front lawn of Baker. "We have to pick up Alison and be at the Holistic Café by five."

* * *

Jane and Dana stopped at two junk shops, a vintage clothing store, and a fancy antique shop as they wound their way through Greenleaf. Finally they got to Laurel's Old Stuff, a funky store upstairs from the Tutti Frutti ice-cream parlor on Main Street.

"I love this place," Jane confided.

"Me, too," Dana said. "When I lived here, it was one of my most surefire cheer-up spots. If I ever got real down in the dumps about something, I could come here and poke through all the old jewelry and postcards and try on these dresses with a million buttons and wide hats with plumes and come out feeling a hundred percent better."

"I especially like coming here on rainy days," Jane said. "It reminds me of going up into the attic in my house in Boston. My father's family has lived there for generations, and so the attic is chock-full of good stuff. I've been up there a hundred times and still haven't gone through half of it."

"I'd love to have a place like that," Dana said, "where I could rummage around in my own past."

"Hmmm," Jane said pensively. "My own past. I never quite thought of it like that. Oh, look here! Aren't these great? Fans." She flipped one open and began fluttering it in front of herself.

"Do you think Alison's the fan type?" Dana wondered.

"It's hard to picture, isn't it?" Jane admitted. "Then she'd have to both push her glasses up *and* fan herself while she was sitting around. It might be too much for her. What about this, though?" Jane held up a feather boa, then wrapped it around Dana's neck and shoulders in a movie-star sweep.

"Do you think boas are big among graduate students?" Dana asked. "You know Alison's going for a master's in art history."

"Yes, she told us. I think it's great. She and David really have things worked out. He really seems like the perfect husband-type guy."

Dana didn't say anything.

"You just met him this morning, I hear," Jane said, now trying on an old band jacket with gold braiding across the front. "What did you think?"

Dana first thought she'd just keep quiet, but then decided to tell Jane about the fight they'd witnessed.

"That really doesn't sound like the David I've seen," was Jane's response when Dana had finished the story. "Do you think this wedding's getting to him?"

"I hope that's all it is," Dana mused, picking up an old stereopticon and looking into the eyepiece. "Hey! Niagara Falls!" she said, and gave the viewer to Jane so she could have a look.

They roamed through the shop like this for half an hour. Laurel, who owned the place, knew Jane well, remembered Dana, and was interested when they told her what their assignment was.

"I think I might have what you're looking for," she said, her eyes twinkling behind her granny glasses. Laurel was not old (only in her late twenties) but everything she wore was. She really got into the spirit of her shop. Now she disappeared into the back of the store and it was several minutes before she emerged again.

"I've been saving this for some time now, for a special occasion," she said, opening an old white box, gone ivory with age. Inside was carefully-folded tissue paper which she opened to reveal a beautiful silk camisole with tiny covered buttons all the way up the front.

"It's over a hundred years old," Laurel told the girls. "It was part of a trousseau someone sold me — a cedar chest full of clothes belonging to another bride from a long time ago."

"Oh, it's so beautiful," Jane sighed.

"And it's perfect for Alison," Dana said.

"Alison Cavanaugh?" Laurel asked. "Is she the bride?"

Both girls nodded.

"Oh, then it's doubly perfect! Alison's been coming in here for years. She really appreciates old things. I can't think of anyone I'd rather have this than her."

"How much?" Dana asked, coming back to the hard ground of financial reality.

"Just give me what you two planned to spend," she said, smiling as she rewrapped the camisole. "Sometimes what I get for an item isn't so important as who it goes to."

Meanwhile Toby wasn't shopping at all. She had the "something borrowed" assignment and so was rummaging through her treasure locker with her flashlight. Finally, from the deepest recesses, she found what she wanted. She held it and smiled, feeling good about loaning Alison something that meant a lot to her. It made her feel more a part of the wedding. She hoped Alison and the others would understand this gift, then decided not to worry about it.

"By now, they all just expect me to be weird," she said aloud to herself, as she slammed the old metal locker door shut and went off to find some wrapping paper.

Shelley didn't really have to shop around, either. As soon as she drew the "something blue" slip, she knew exactly what she was going to get Alison.

She knew that Alison and David were planning to take a delayed honeymoon over the Christmas holidays. They were going to Jamaica. Ever since Shelley had seen a magazine article on Caribbean reefs — like gorgeous underwater discos where the most brilliantly-colored fish hung out — she had dreamed of going down there to snorkel. She loved thinking that Alison would really have the chance to do this, and wanted to make sure she was properly outfitted. She was determined to find some flippers, a mask, and snorkel — in blue, of course. She laughed to herself, thinking she was lucky the rhyme went the way it did. If it had been *something borrowed, something purple*, she would have had a much harder job. She'd never seen purple flippers. But she was fairly certain she'd be able to find some blue ones at Dugan's Sporting Goods in town.

She pushed open the door of the store, setting off a tiny bell that brought a salesgirl out of the back. When she saw who this salesgirl was, Shelley's jaw dropped. It was Cynthia, Tom's new girl friend!

Today she was wearing a blouse with teddy bears printed all over it. There was something "goody-two-shoes" about her that made Shelley wince. No one older than nine could be this sweet.

She recognized Shelley right away and said hi, then asked what she could help her with.

She didn't seem at all flustered or bothered. Which rankled Shelley a little. It probably meant Tom had told her Shelley was someone he'd taken driver training with.

"Uh," Shelley started, trying to be cool, "I'm just looking for some snorkeling equipment."

"Oh," Cynthia said.

"You *do* carry snorkeling equipment, don't you?" Shelley said, arching an eyebrow. "I mean, this *is* a sporting goods store, isn't it?"

"Y-y-y-yes," Cynthia began stammering, "b-b-b-but it's kind of out of season."

Shelley felt bad for making Cynthia nervous to the point of stuttering. And for blustering in here with what was probably a slightly outrageous demand. Of course there wouldn't be a big display of snorkeling equipment in late November. What had she been thinking of?

"B-b-b-but I can go down to the stockroom and look for what you need. It just may take a while. Wait here."

She was almost through the doorway to the back of the store when Shelley called out after her, "Why don't you let me help you look?"

Cynthia turned, looked intently at Shelley, and said, "You *are* as nice as Tom said."

When they got to the bottom of the old stairs, they faced a huge, musty basement full of balls and bats and rackets and boxes and caps and goalie masks and croquet wickets. The whole place was a giant jumble.

"Oh, my," Shelley said.

"I know," Cynthia said. "It's quite a mess. And mostly my doing. It's only taken me a couple of weeks to get the place in this sorry shape. Since my uncle had his heart attack. It's his store. Me and my mom and dad are just pitching in until Uncle Bert gets back on his feet. I come in after school and all day Saturdays."

"That's really nice of you," Shelley said.

"Oh, I'm not so sure. I'm probably losing him money. I don't know a thing about sports. I'm always trying to sell badminton rackets to tennis players and hockey sticks to golfers."

"No," Shelley said.

"Well, not quite that bad," Cynthia admitted, "but nearly. And as you can see, I've just about totaled this stockroom. My uncle could probably collect cyclone insurance."

Shelley had to laugh. "Cynthia, do you think you could give me a general area to start looking around in?"

Cynthia looked doubtful as she surveyed the room, and finally all she could come up with was, "Well, I found some noseplugs over in that corner last week. That might be a promising area."

But it turned out to be a false lead and the two girls, with Cynthia rushing upstairs every time the bell announced another customer, took nearly an hour before they came up with a mask and snorkel and a pair of fins. Well, not exactly a pair. One was blue, the other green.

"Kind of like a lot of my socks," Cynthia confessed.

"You don't really wear mismatched pairs, do you?" Shelley asked.

"My family doesn't have much money," Cynthia said, parceling the words out carefully, as if they were hard to say. "I'm afraid I wear a lot of mismatched socks. And clothes that come in the mail from relatives."

Shelley instantly felt awful for all her snide comments about Cynthia. She hadn't thought there might be anything behind her lack of style besides lack of taste. And then she felt even worse when it occurred to her that what she'd been doing to Cynthia was just what Jane Barrett had been doing to her, when she looked at Shelley as if she fully expected her to be chewing on a piece of hay.

"Did Tom really tell you I'm nice?" Shelley asked Cynthia, embarrassed now at having been rude, not living up to the good words Tom had been saying about her. The two of them were sitting on a large carton marked CATCHER'S MITTS. Shelley had taken off her shoes and put the flippers on over her socks. Cynthia had pulled the mask and snorkel over her face, so her reply was a little muffled.

"He said you're so great that if you still lived out here, he would never have come looking for me."

"He said *that*, did he? Hmm."

"I'm really glad he did come looking for me, though. I really love Tom, you know," Cynthia said. "He makes me laugh all the time and not mind so much when the going gets rough. And he really lets me know he loves me . . . and doesn't care if he looks foolish doing it."

Shelley nodded, thinking of Tom bringing Cynthia that little wild-flower bouquet. She could see now that she hadn't really hated the gesture because it was dumb, but because she was jealous that Cynthia brought out this open, unguardedly goofy side of Tom that Shelley hadn't. But then, if anyone could bring out openness and goofiness, it was Cynthia in her hand-me-down teddy bear blouse and ear-to-ear smile.

"You know," Shelley told her, making fishy motions in front of the glass of the mask, "at first I thought you must be unreal, that no one could be as nice as you are. But you really are."

"Everyone says that. Sometime I'll surprise them all. I'll throw a big tantrum in the middle of Main Street."

"Oh, no," Shelley moaned, "don't. Stay just the way you are. We need all the niceness we can get around here." Especially this week, she thought. With all the lions, the old ones and the new, gathered in 407, sitting on their little stands, swatting at each other with their paws.

But two of the lions had *stopped* swatting. Andy and Faith. Neither knew quite how it had happened. Or when. But it was at the mall, somewhere between the music box shop and the Chinese fast food stand, where they were sitting now at a small table sharing an order of egg rolls. Maybe it had been one or another of the jokes that got transmitted instantly between them. They'd found they shared the *exact* same sense of humor.

Maybe it had been their talk about Andy's ballet and Faith's photography, their plans for lives as committed artists, whatever the struggles and odds against them. Maybe it had just been the long, funny talk they'd had about life with brothers. Faith had one, Andy two. Whatever it had been that undid all the knots between them, it happened before either of them had noticed it happening. And brought them to where they were now, eating egg rolls and beginning to talk about the one thing they still had to talk about.

"Look," Andy said. "I'm sorry I jumped all over you the other day."

"You *were* a little rough," Faith said. "But then, afterward, I realized I hadn't told you the whole truth. I wasn't thinking back far enough. I wasn't thinking way back to my first days here when Canby Hall seemed like a sea of white faces and I was sure Shelley hated me because I was black. Things got a lot better from there, though."

"And from then on you never had anyone act like you were from a different planet?" Andy said.

"Oh, sure. It still happens sometimes. Even now."

"But mostly you don't feel any different anymore?"

"Mostly no one *makes* me feel different. But my own awareness is always up. Being black is fundamental to who I am. And I think it's important for our white friends to see our differences from them in a positive way. That's why I've been doing so much work on the Black History Week committee at school."

"You have?" Andy said. "Boy, that makes me feel even worse about all my crummy remarks."

"Oh, don't. They set me to thinking, which was good. I'm not perfect. When you told me you've been having trouble here, I should have rallied behind you, not gotten on your case."

"Aw," Andy said, now embarrassed.

"And tell Gigi Norton that if she so much as looks cross-eyed at you while I'm around, she's going to find out firsthand about my expertise in the martial arts."

"Are you really an expert?"

"No," Faith said, smiling, "but some girls are easy to fool about stuff like that. They're never quite sure what tricks we've learned in the inner city."

The two of them laughed and talked all the way over to Sears, where they headed for the housewares floor. They were going to survey the possibilities among small appliances. After looking over the waffle iron and electric wok and coffee grinders, they stumbled onto the perfect gift for Alison.

"Oh, look!" said Andy, who was the first to spot it being demonstrated.

"Yes, girls," the demonstrator woman said, "it's the latest in kitchen wizardry: the talking toaster! Just put in a slice of bread and when it's done, it not only pops up, but — "

And here an electronic voice came on and said, "Your toast is done."

"And now see what happens if you put in a bagel half like this and it's too fat and gets stuck," the woman demonstrated, pointing at the toaster. It was now emitting a small cloud of black smoke and speaking electronically, saying smugly, "You've burnt your toast."

"Oh, this is great!" Faith said. "Superb."

"The perfect gift for the world's most incompetent cook. We have to get it."

While they were standing at the counter, waiting for the saleswoman to gift wrap the toaster, Faith pressed an elbow into Andy's ribs and whispered, "Don't look like you're looking," she said, "but there's Michael."

"Where?"

"Over there, looking at the coffee makers."

Andy couldn't resist turning around to look, and was instantly spotted by Michael, who came over, holding the coffee maker he was apparently buying.

"Hi, Andy. Hey, *Faith*," he said smiling. "I didn't know you were in town. How come you haven't been by to see me?"

"Oh, well, you know, me and Dana and Shelley . . ." Faith sputtered, not knowing what to say.

"Ahhh," Michael said, raising his eyebrows to show he got the picture, "the wedding."

"Yeah, we're just buying her this toaster," Andy interjected, trying to move the conversation to more neutral ground. "It talks."

"The toaster?" Michael said, as if he'd misunderstood.

Both girls nodded, laughing.

"What does it say?" he teased. "To be or not to be? $E = MC^2$?"

"Come *on*, Michael," Andy said.

"It tells you your toast is done," Faith said.

"What an important invention!" Michael said sarcastically. "Absolutely vital to mankind! Now we no longer have to rely on visual estimation of toast readiness!"

"All right, all right," Faith protested, "so it's dumb. But you've got to admit it'll appeal to Alison's sense of humor."

At this first direct mention of her name, the smile fell from Michael's lips. Faith was instantly sorry she'd said it.

"Oh, Michael. . . ." She started to say she was sorry, putting a hand on his arm. But he shrugged it off and looked at his watch.

"I've got to run. I'm late," he said, not very convincingly. The saleswoman handed him his package and he managed to give Faith and Andy a quick, "Good seeing you," before lurching off toward the exit with long determined strides, his shoulders stooped dejectedly.

When he'd gone, Andy turned to Faith and said, "Did you see what he was buying? It was so sad."

"No. What was it?"

"A Mr. Coffee for *one*."

CHAPTER FOURTEEN

By five-thirty, all six girls had wrapped their gifts, showered, changed into their casual best, and were walking along the old country road that led to the Holistic Café. They had told Alison the shower was at six, and wanted to get there early to make sure everything was ready and just right.

Seeing them, a passerby might wonder what connected six girls with such dramatically different styles. Toby was wearing her boots with the snakeskin inserts, along with black jeans and a black Western shirt with white piping. The effect, especially contrasted with her red hair, was striking.

Andy had on army green wool slacks with deep pleats, and an oversized cream-colored wool sweater. Dana had decided on a skirt and sweater combination in dusty rose set off by cordovan boots. Faith had picked a red wool

dress with black tights. Shelley was wearing
pale green cords and a boatneck sweater with
a geometric print across the front in many
colors. Jane, of course, was the preppiest of
the lot in pressed khakis and a navy cashmere
turtleneck.

Underlying their differences in style were
remaining differences in personality. Jane had
already made a sly remark about Shelley's
weird-looking package (the absolute best
wrapping job she could do on flippers and a
snorkel). Toby was still a little wary of Dana
because of her disrupting effect on Randy.
But they *were* a more peaceful and harmo-
nious group tonight than they had been before. Faith and Andy had gone from being
deadly enemies to nearly friends. The afternoon's shopping had given Jane and Dana
something in common. Toby and Shelley were
talking now about all the fun they had had at
state fairs and 4-H events.

One subject, though, on which they split
into their old warring camps was David Gordon. The three younger girls were all sold on
him now. He'd been so good-natured about
their stunt in the movie theater. And afterward, he'd been so charming and funny at the
Tutti Frutti, not to mention picking up the
bill for everyone's sundaes! And they all liked
seeing how sweet he and Alison were with
each other, teasing like playful, cuffing bears.

The older girls, though, had seen only one moment of David, and that moment included only two things: his shouting at Alison, and then storming off in a huff. They had very little to go on, and it was all negative. Everything had been such a rush today that the three of them hadn't had a chance to talk about the incident. But when the younger girls started singing David's praises, Faith, Dana, and Shelley found they had each separately come to the same conclusion.

Dana was the first one to say it aloud. "Alison should get out of this wedding."

"I've just been thinking the very same thing," Shelley said.

"Me, too," Faith added. "I was going along with it, even the fact that she had to dump poor Michael in the process. Anyway, I figured the whole thing was her business. But then this morning, I finally got to meet the wonderful David Gordon." She turned to the younger girls and added, "Frankly, I think he was just turning on the charm for you last night. I think the way he acted this morning, when he didn't know he had an audience, gives a better picture of what he's *really* like."

"I agree," Shelley said. "But what are we going to do about it, or, more to the point, about poor Alison?"

"I don't know what we *can* do," Dana said. "The wedding's less than twenty-four hours away. Big events have their own momentum.

I mean, even if Cleopatra had wanted to stop her grand entrance into Rome and go out for some spaghetti instead, by the time that procession got going, she was probably pretty well locked into the situation. I think Alison's our Cleopatra. It's probably too late to rescue her."

"I hardly think rescuing would be an appropriate measure," Jane said huffily. "Alison invited you three here to celebrate her wedding, and now you're trying to undermine her confidence in her decision. I sometimes wonder what kind of friends you really are."

"*Caring* friends," Shelley snapped. "Not just party pals. Remember, you three didn't see the side of David we saw this morning."

"And *you*," Jane said, glaring straight at Shelley, "did not see what we saw of him last night. How can we know who got the truer impression?"

"We can't," Toby said, supportively.

"That's right," Andy said, giving Faith a tug on the sleeve. "And so we've got to go in there and make this the best shower that's ever happened. For tonight, we've got to forget the groom. This is a party strictly for the bride!"

The others thought and nodded. As much as they differed in their opinions of David, they were unanimous in their feeling for Alison. They wanted to make her happy, and so let this argument go for the moment. They began making final plans for the shower — what tapes they'd brought, when they'd give her their gifts, what they'd sing when the cake came out.

While this discussion went on, Dana tugged on the back of Faith's jacket to signal her to drop behind the others. When the rest of the girls had gone on ahead, she turned to Faith and said, "About Michael. Do you think you could go and talk to him? See if he's okay? I think of all the times we leaned on him, and now he's in pain, and we're off dancing at the wedding."

Faith nodded. "I'm gathering you don't want to come with me?" Faith said.

Dana shook her head. "I'm afraid I'd start blubbering and only make him feel worse. Plus I'd feel a little like a traitor — standing up for Alison tomorrow, and consoling her old boyfriend tonight. Besides, you'll do better at this than I would."

"All right," Faith agreed. "I'll go. But he may not want to talk with me. What I saw out at the mall was a guy who's dug himself a deep hole and wants to sit down there for a while. And he may want to do his sitting alone."

When the six of them came around the bend and found themselves in front of the Holistic Café, there was someone standing in the doorway. A guy with longish curly hair, tiny horn-rimmed sunglasses (in spite of the fact that the sun was nearly down), and an earring in his left ear.

"Must be one of the weird types that hang out here," Dana said.

"Oh, I'm afraid it's not," Jane said, slightly embarrassed. "I'm afraid it's my boyfriend."

"My," Dana said. "He's . . . well . . . he's not exactly who I'd expect you to be involved with."

"Me, either," Jane said. "It surprises me all the time. And at the moment, I'm not sure I *am* involved with him. He's boycotting this wedding because it's so traditional and middle-class and boring. I've no idea what he's doing here."

Jane got a better idea when Cary smiled and asked if he could see her alone for a minute before she went in.

"How did you even find me out here?" she wondered.

"My vast intelligence network," he bluffed. When Jane stared him down, though, he relented and said, "Dee answered your phone and told me."

He put an arm over her shoulder and walked her around into the little arbor behind the restaurant. When they stood beneath the lattice of tree branches, the thin, late afternoon sun dappling across their shoulders, he took both her hands in his and look her in the eyes.

"I've been a dope," he said. "I was so high

up on my high horse. What matters is that you're going to this wedding, and that you want me there with you. So please, Jane, tell me you'll forgive me."

"Of course . . ." Jane said, intending to follow up with, "but I've asked someone else."

But Cary leaned in to kiss her too soon. She didn't have a chance to finish her sentence. And then, before she knew it, he was running off down the road, stopping only to do ballet jumps and to shout, "I'm going to dance all night!"

Oh, oh, Jane thought. What have I done?

By the time she caught up with the others, they were already bustling around the restaurant's private upstairs dining room, putting the finishing touches on the shower.

Toby and Andy were draping the table in crepe paper streamers in Alison's favorite color, purple. Faith was tacking up Canby Hall photos she'd taken over the years. Shelley was setting up her portable stereo and loading it with a Bob Seger tape, one of Alison's big favorites. Dana and Faith were talking with Harvey, the owner, about the dinner and cake.

By six o'clock they were all standing at the door, poised to spring out at Alison when she came through. Which she did within minutes, on time for once in her life. And she looked stunning, more sophisticated than the girls had ever seen her, in beige raw silk slacks and a rust-colored sweater. The girls were used to her in hodgepodge outfits, layers of tights and skirts and turtlenecks and shawls. This new tailored, crisp look caused them all to take a new look at Alison, to really realize that she was going through a major life change. Soon she was no longer going to be their funky housemother, but a graduate student and the wife of a media personality. She was going to have a very different life from the one she'd been living at Canby Hall. And she was probably going to change as a result of it. Tonight, they all knew they were seeing the first of the new Alison, which was exciting. But also sad as it meant they were also seeing the last of the old Alison.

As all the girls swarmed around her, enveloping her in hugs, tears streamed down Alison's face, fogging her glasses and making them slide down her nose even faster than usual.

"Oh, this is so wonderful. I've never had a shower before," she cried. "It's so much fun."

"Alison," Dana said, "we haven't even started. We've got so many treats in store for you tonight. . . . Well, come in, let's start. First of all, sit down here at the head of the table and look at your special menu." Dana handed Alison a card with hand-done calligraphy (Faith's contribution). It read:

Alison's Girls
Present
A Bridal Dinner

Appetizer
Guacamole Casa Baker
Soup
Mushroom Bisque à la Canby Hall
Salad
Greenleaf Leafy Greens
Entree
Spaghetti Cavanaugh
Dessert
Penthouse Cake

"Oh, this is just too much," Alison sighed, pressing the card to her chest as two waitresses started bringing out the guacamole and corn chips. Midway through this course, Alison's tear-fogged glasses cleared and she saw for the first time Faith's photos on the walls. She got up from her chair and walked around the room, peering at each one closely, exclaiming.

"Oh, remember this!? The Maple Syrup Festival! Oh, and here, that dreadful production of *Macbeth*, with Pamela Young hamming it up with her 'Out damned spot!' like she was going for an Oscar. Oh, and here's the day I found Doby. He was so little then, but with such big ears! Oh, Faith, these are great."

"Keep them. I made the whole set of prints for you. You can show all your new friends in

Boston that you had this bout of temporary insanity . . . living at Canby Hall!" Faith said.

The others laughed and the soup arrived and everyone, old and new girls alike, started talking about what it was like to be a Canby Hall girl.

"I think we're really different from kids who live at home and go to regular high schools," Jane said.

"Oh, definitely," Toby agreed. "We have more jokes. We probably have closer friends. I think we get to fool around more."

"Right," Andy agreed. "No parents around all the time looking over our shoulders, bossing us around, telling us what to do."

"Yes," Faith said, "but the fact that no grown-ups are looking over your shoulder makes you have to be more grown-up yourself."

"You're not kidding," Shelley said. "I can remember the first few weeks I was here. I was so used to my mother doing my laundry that I just let everything run out. I guess I thought some elves would do it, or something. But then three days in the same pair of socks, and I suddenly got very into doing my own wash."

"And it's not just laundry and practical stuff," Toby added. "When I lived on the ranch, I could hardly brush my teeth without checking first with my dad. Now I've got to think a lot of important things through by myself, and then go with my own decisions on them. I think being here makes us a lot more independent than most kids our age."

"Yeah," Jane said, "but on the down side, we do not get tucked in at night."

"Jane!" Andy shouted. "Your mother still tucks you in?! I don't believe it. Then I suppose it must also make you sad that Baker House only has showers."

"Why would it make me sad?" Jane asked earnestly, not seeing the joke coming.

"Because you haven't got a tub to float your rubber ducky in," Andy quipped.

Everybody laughed at this, even Jane.

By the time they got to dessert, all the girls felt a little closer than they had before. Whatever their differences, they all shared the experience of Canby Hall, which would forever make them different from other girls . . . and connected to each other.

It was Andy and Faith who got up and went back into the kitchen, waiting there until Dana switched the lights off in the small dining room before they came out with a huge chocolate cake aglow with candles. By prearrangement, this was everyone's cue to burst into the corniest possible rendition of "For she's a jolly good housemom" ever heard. Alison groaned at this off-key tribute, but was clearly enjoying the attention.

They brought out their presents, which put

Alison through new waves of emotion. A sigh at the beauty of Jane and Dana's something old.

"It's so Victorian," Alison said, holding the camisole up against herself. "I'll have to splash rosewater on my shoulders every time I wear it."

Then she was moved to laughter at the wrapping job on Shelley's something blue.

"I've always wanted to snorkel, though," she said when she'd taken the wrap off. "Now I'm all set."

Next she opened Faith and Andy's something new, the toaster, and erupted into laughter again.

"I'm so absentminded, I should have talking everythings. A talking pillow that says, 'Get up — and I mean it!' A talking toothbrush that says, 'Be sure to get those molars.' "

She opened Toby's gift last.

"You've got something old, something new, and something blue," Toby said, awkwardly handing over a small box. "Now all you need is something borrowed. This is the best thing I have to lend you."

"Sure is heavy," Alison said, her hand dropping with the sudden weight in it. When she undid the tissue paper, inside was a rusty metal "U."

"It's my lucky horseshoe," Toby explained. "I figure people getting married need all the luck they can get."

"But what makes it lucky?" Alison wondered, turning it over in her hands.

"Well . . ." Toby started, "I was standing in the corral one day and our meanest horse, Ivan — we call him that because he's so terrible — he was fussing and fuming about something and threw a loose shoe off one of his hind hooves. It came at me at about a hundred miles an hour, and missed me by half an inch. I figured not getting killed then and there was about the luckiest thing that ever happened to me. And so I saved the shoe. Now you can borrow it for tomorrow. For your wedding."

Alison looked down at the horseshoe for a long time before she handed it back to Toby.

"Maybe you shouldn't loan it to me," she said finally. "I've been thinking all through this shower about how much I love Canby Hall, and my life here. How much I'll miss all of you. I keep wondering why I'm leaving. I keep thinking of how awful David was this morning, and how I probably didn't look enough before I leaped into this marriage. And so I think I'd better postpone this wedding."

"Maybe you should, Alison," Dana said gently. She felt she was only encouraging Alison to think a little longer. But Jane saw her advice in a different light.

"Stop interfering," she told Dana sharply.

"I'm not interfering," Dana defended herself. "I'm only trying to be supportive. If Alison wants to change her mind about getting married tomorrow, I just want her to know I'll be there for her."

"But she doesn't know *what* she wants anymore," said Andy, who was David's biggest fan among the girls, and so was not crazy about this talk of postponing the wedding. Plus she was getting irritated with Dana for meddling. She felt a hand on her arm. It was Faith, trying to calm her down. But Andy pulled away. Right now she didn't *want* to be calmed down. She wanted to make her point.

She turned to Alison and said, "This is all just last-minute nervousness on both your and David's part."

Alison looked up at Andy hopefully, and said, "I wish I could be sure that was all it was. I'm so confused. My head's a jumble of doubts."

"Of course it is," Jane said soothingly. "I imagine anyone's is the night before her wedding."

"I don't think that's necessarily true," said Faith, who was increasingly skeptical about this marriage. "I think Alison may have some real issues here, and you and Andy aren't letting her deal with them. You just keep patting her on the head and telling her everything's going to be fine."

"Faith's right," Shelley said, backing up her old friend. "This isn't just a *wedding* we're talking about. It's a *marriage*. It's the rest of Alison's life!"

Suddenly Alison put her hands to her head and shouted, "Would everyone please stop talking about me as if I'm not here? As though I'm a child who can't make her own decisions." She stopped, and when she spoke again, it was much more softly, barely above a whisper.

"I need to be alone for a while," she said, getting up from the table, gathering up her jacket and bag, and muttering to herself as she rushed out the door, "I need to think!"

CHAPTER FIFTEEN

After Alison had run out of the room, the girls all sat silent for a moment, then burst into a din of unanswerable questions.

"Do you think she really meant it, about postponing the wedding?" Toby asked.

"Where did she run off to?" Jane wondered.

"To talk to David?" Andy said.

"To see Michael?" Faith hoped aloud.

"To Rio to hide out for a while?" said Shelley, who watched the soaps, where people often took off for Rio when they needed to think things over.

"Do you think she's all right?" Dana asked, concerned.

"What should we do?" Faith asked.

"Should we try to find her?" Shelley wondered.

"I don't think so," said Dana, who knew Alison best. "I think we ought to leave her alone right now. She needs a little room to breathe." She turned suddenly and looked straight at Andy, Toby, and Jane and said, "Which means you shouldn't bother her."

"I don't know *what* you're insinuating," Jane replied haughtily, "but you can be assured none of us would even *think* of bothering Alison. It's *you* three who've come to town and gotten her all riled up."

"Just what are you saying?" Shelley asked defensively.

"Well . . ." Jane said, pretending to be more interested in examining the polish on her nails, "before you arrived on the scene and started agitating her, she and David were Bill and Coo, the little lovebirds. Now the wedding's off and she's a complete wreck. Draw your own conclusions."

This remark had the effect of inciting a battle that began with shouting, progressed to name calling and accusation hurling, and wound up with Shelley grabbing a large chocolaty hunk of cake and pushing it in the extremely astonished face of Jane Barrett.

At about this point, Harvey, the owner of the café, came in and put an abrupt end to the party. Toby helped Jane wash most of the frosting out of her hair in the ladies' room while the others gathered up the presents Alison had left behind, and what was left of the demolished cake, and hurried out of the restaurant.

They walked back to campus in a silence that was a combination of anger, embarrassment, and frustration at being so divided on the issue of Alison and the wedding. There really wasn't anything more to say on the subject. Andy, Toby, and Jane thought David was great and Alison should get over her nervousness and marry him. Faith, Dana, and Shelley had varying degrees of doubt about David, but all thought Alison was under too much pressure. In addition, Faith and Dana secretly hoped Alison would go back to Michael, whom they knew and loved.

As soon as they walked into Baker House, the night receptionist handed Jane a package.

"It's addressed to 'The Old Girls of 407' — whatever that means," the receptionist said.

"Must be you three," Jane said, icily handing the package over to Dana, who ripped open the brown paper to reveal a videocassette.

"What is it, do you think?" Shelley said.

"And where are we going to play it?" Faith asked.

"Meredith Wade has a VCR in her room. Her father's in oil. Meredith gets everything she wants." Jane had no interest in helping the old girls, but had a large curiosity about what was on the tape, and so was trying to find them a place to see it.

"But Meredith is so selfish," Andy said.

"That's true," Jane admitted. "She's not big on lending or sharing. But at the moment, she's trying to be *very* nice to me. I fixed her up a couple of weeks ago with this friend of Neal's. She's nutty about this guy, thinks he's off the edge of the cute scale. She wants me to get Neal to bring him out again. So I think she'll let us use her machine to play this. She'll probably even offer to run the tape for us."

She did.

As Meredith punched the play button, the others sat silently on the floor in front of her tv, watching as the screen went from black to the set of *Nighttime News*, with David sitting as usual behind the big white formica desk. Something was *not* as usual, though. They all picked up on it, but Andy was the first one to catch exactly what was different.

"He's not wearing a jacket and tie, just a polo shirt, the same one he was wearing at breakfast this morning."

By now, the camera had closed in on his face as he stared seriously into the lens.

"Good evening. I'm David Gordon and this is *Nighttime News*. Tonight's top story: Anchorman behaves like total jerk. At precisely ten-seventeen this morning, Gordon, usually a wonderful person, flew off the handle at his beloved fianceé, Alison Cavanaugh, thereby embarrassing her in front of three of her friends — Dana Morrison, Faith Thompson, and Shelley Hyde — who had probably never seen such a childish tantrum performed by an adult. They are suspected to now have grave doubts on the suitability of Gordon as a husband for Cavanaugh, their beloved housemother. Cavanaugh herself has been unavailable for comment.

"When interviewed, Gordon said that he is extremely sorry, and that he ardently, sincerely, and desperately looks forward to a wonderful lifetime with Cavanaugh, *if* she'll still have him and *if* they can get through the wedding, which is proving slightly more demanding than climbing the Himalayas.

"From Morrison, Thompson, and Hyde, he asks only another chance."

"Well, he *is* kind of cute," Shelley said as the tape lapsed into staticky flecks.

"And it *is* a pretty impressive apology," Dana admitted.

"Could just be media hype, though," Faith said cynically. "I mean, sounding sincere on tv is what this guy's paid to do, after all."

"Maybe you're right," Dana said.

"Well, *I* believe him," Jane said. "Why would he go to the trouble to make the tape unless he really *is* sorry?"

"He could just be trying to save his pride," Faith said. "I know *I* wouldn't want people going around thinking I was a big jerk. He probably doesn't, either. So he puts together this charming little tape and sends it along. But does it really *mean* anything? Does it mean he'll never throw another tantrum? Me,

I prefer guys who don't *have* to make cute apologies because they don't act like brats in the first place. Guys like my guy, Johnny. Michael Frank's that kind of guy, too." She thought for a moment, then clapped Dana lightly on the shoulder and said, "I think I'll go see him now. Get an idea of where *he* fits in this picture."

"Where are the three of us going to sleep tonight?" Shelley wondered aloud. "I don't think we ought to barge into The Penthouse, in case Alison wants her privacy."

"We can bunk in with my sister," Dana said. "Snag some pillows and spend another comfy night on the floor."

Faith took off to find Michael and the others trooped up to the fourth floor together, silent, angry, thinking their individual thoughts. Jane was astonished at herself when, in the middle of thinking truly concerned thoughts about Alison, it crossed her mind that the wedding being called off would at least save her from the dilemma of having inadvertently invited two dates. She was instantly ashamed at being so selfish, and made up her mind to begin work tomorrow on being a better person, the kind of person who wouldn't even think a thought like that.

As the five of them came down the fourth floor hallway together, they could hear a phone ringing and ringing and ringing.

"Boy," Toby said, whistling low, "someone

must really want to get in touch with someone."

When they got closer, they could tell the
ringing was coming from the phone in 407.
Jane thought it might be Cary. Andy thought
it might be Matt. Toby thought it might be,
but probably wasn't, Randy.

But it was. The only thing was, he wasn't
calling for Toby. And unfortunately, she was
the one who reached the phone first and
picked it up.

"Hi, Toby."

"Randy!"

"How're you doing?"

"Oh, fine. Just fine. Well, not really. It
looks like Alison's calling off the wedding."

"Eleventh-hour nerves?" he asked.

"Huh?"

"Is she getting cold feet?"

"No, it's more like she's got a hot head.
She's mad at David."

"They might still work it out."

"I hope so," Toby said. "I really like him."
She didn't know what to say next. It was so
unusual for him to call. "How's Maxine?" she
tried. One subject they both always found easy
was horse talk.

"Oh, fine," he said, but distractedly, then
quickly followed with, "Listen, I'm sorry to
bother you with this, but I'm looking for
Dana. I tried calling Alison's, but there's no
answer. I thought you all might be together."

"We are," Toby said, hurt. "I mean she is." And in an embarrassed attempt to just get off the line, she signaled Dana to come into the room and said, "Here," handing her the receiver.

Mercifully, the conversation was short. Toby only had to listen to Dana say, "Hi. . . . Okay. . . . All right. . . . Of course. . . . No, I understand. . . . In ten minutes, then. . . . 'Bye."

When she'd hung up, she silently pulled Toby further into 407 so they could have a moment's privacy.

"Listen, I'm sorry," Dana started to say, but Toby stopped her.

"No, it's okay. If there's something still happening between the two of you, you ought to talk about it. Otherwise, you'll both wonder about it forever."

"Either you really are just Randy's friend, or you're the most generous-spirited girl I've ever met."

"Neither," Toby said softly. "Just Texas-sensible. I don't have him yet, and I'll never get him if he's still pining away for you. Now, if you'll excuse me, I think I'll just head down to the broom closet for a little while so I can be alone with my thoughts. As they say . . . even cowgirls get the blues sometimes."

The broom closet was the only place on the fourth floor where a girl could get total privacy, and so there was usually someone in there at any given moment, sitting among the mops and buckets and vacuum cleaners. Usually the broom closet inhabitant was crying, but sometimes she was just deep in thought, pondering the eternal truths of the universe, but more often brooding over some guy.

Dana felt awful letting Toby go off by herself, but didn't know what to say to stop her. And so it was with mixed feelings that she went downstairs to meet Randy out in front of Baker House.

She stood there for ten minutes before she heard the wild rattle of his ancient pick-up coming down the road. She watched as it approached through the campus gates and up the drive. When he got to where she was standing, he put on the brakes and threw open the door on the passenger side of the cab.

"Hop on in," he shouted over the noise of the motor.

She got in and they both smiled tentatively at each other, but didn't say anything. He turned the radio up and they listened to an oldies show as they drove out a back road, all the way to Hudson's Creek.

In summer, the creek was Greenleaf's favorite swimming spot. Now it was deserted, the banks covered in fallen leaves, the waters rushing by, silvery with moonlight.

Randy pulled the truck up onto the bank overlooking the creek and killed the engine. He sat looking straight ahead through the windshield for a long moment, as if gathering his thoughts into the right words.

Finally he turned to Dana and said, "I'm sorry about the other day. I just felt so close to you, like old times, that I guess I lost my head."

"Apology accepted," Dana said. "I've wanted to call you, but I couldn't think of exactly what to say. You see, the thing is, I feel some of the old stuff happening again between us, too. What does it mean?"

He shook his head. "I'm not sure. I thought you were all through with me long before you left this place."

"This place," Dana said, sighing and looking out over the waters. "The funny thing is that I left thinking, Oh, wow! Graduation! I'm off to Hawaii! And it *has* been fun living on the island. A really different experience. And I like getting to spend some time with my dad. But lately I've been feeling more and more lonely. . . . And then coming out here for the wedding, well . . . I guess I've been missing Greenleaf and Canby Hall more than I knew."

"But coming back for a weekend like this," Randy said, "it's so full of nostalgia. You might just be feeling a brief flash of something. If you really lived here again, don't you think you'd miss the bright lights of Broadway, those galleries in Soho you told me about,

your favorite Thai restaurant? Don't you
think you might get a little bored with coming
back to a social life centered on the Tutti
Frutti and Pizza Pete's?"

"But you don't find it boring here," she
challenged him.

"No, but my real world is out here, fields
and trees and sunsets and springtime. And
horses. You're a dyed-in-the-wool city girl,
Dana. My guess is you'll eventually wind up
back in Manhattan. You like the pace. You'd
miss it if you stayed away forever. I think that
was one of the problems between us — that
I'm so much of a country boy and you're so
much of a city girl."

Dana had to laugh. "You seem to be trying
real hard to talk me out of coming back, or
even liking you."

He smiled. She watched him. She had always loved that slow, easy smile.

"I just don't want you being swept away
by memories and pretty fall colors and other
people's wedding bells."

"I think," she said, suddenly shy, "that
more bells are ringing right here tonight than
they are around the wedding."

And then, to turn the tables a little, she
leaned across the cab and kissed him.

"Does that mean you're coming back,
Dana?" he said softly.

She pulled back across the front seat, pressing her cheek against the glass of the window, and said, "It means I've got some thinking to do."

At this same moment, back on campus, Faith was sitting in the kitchen of Michael Frank's faculty house, watching him make cocoa.

"The secret is you've got to use the old-fashioned stuff — none of this instant business. The stuff our mothers used to make."

"My mother works full-time," Faith said. "She uses instant everything."

"Well, your grandmother, then."

"She was a lawyer. But I think my grandfather used to make lemonade with real lemons. Do I get a point for that?"

"Not only a point," Michael said, setting two mugs down on the old pine table, "but a cookie to boot." He pulled a package of vanilla wafers down from one of the cabinets.

"The old-fashioned kind," Faith teased. "You must've spent all afternoon whipping these up. And you didn't even know I was coming by."

"I'm glad you did, though," Michael said, sitting down across the table from her. "Afterward, I felt stupid for running out of the store like that. I'm happy we're getting another chance to talk."

When Faith didn't say anything after this, they both had to laugh.

"Or at least a chance to have some hot

chocolate with you. I was just saying to myself the other day, 'I wish Faith Thompson would come back from Rochester and have a cup of hot chocolate with me.' Hey. How's it going in beautiful upstate New York?"

"Pretty good," she said, and detailed her recent triumphs and a couple of the rough spots. Most of her teachers liked her strongly individualistic photography and she'd already been featured in one show at the university gallery, with the New York show coming up. She was, however, close to flunking Spanish.

"It's not that it's even hard," she said. "I'm just not putting the time in. I just can't stand memorizing."

He nodded understandingly. "I nearly flunked French myself. Try setting up a reward equation. Memorize X many verbs and you get X treat."

"Might work," she said, then stopped abruptly. "But wait. We're not here to discuss *my* problems."

"What are we here to discuss?" he said with a teasing look in his eyes. "Someone else's problems? I don't think we ought to do that behind their back."

"Michael. Come on. Talk to me."

"But about what?" he said and laughed.

"Everybody knows you're in the depths of despair over Alison. After all the times I cried on your shoulder, I want you to feel free to cry on mine now."

He looked at her seriously and said, "Sorry to be dry-eyed, but I'm not in the depths of anything. I'm happy for Alison. I think she's got the right guy in David. The three of us went out to dinner together last week and they're perfect for each other."

"And you two weren't?" Faith challenged.

"Not really," he said simply. "Not recently, anyway. We started off great guns, but the romance kind of fizzled out over time. I think mainly we were staying together because we both worked here and so much of our lives were tied up with Canby Hall. And neither of us had anyone else on the scene. Now we do."

"You mean you've got someone new, too?"

He put a hand over his mouth to cover a grin.

"Michael, you sneak. Here I come all the way over here, intent on doing my duty as a friend. And all the while you've got some terrific new romance and don't need any consolation at all."

"Oh, Faith," he mocked her. "Please forgive me for not being miserable."

"Well, I didn't mean it that way, of course," she said, "but wait a minute. If you're really not miserable, how come you've been looking so woebegone? Everyone's noticed."

In response to this, he opened his mouth and pointed inside.

"I had all four of my wisdom teeth pulled last week. I was the most miserable creature on campus, that's for sure. But it didn't have anything to do with love — only dentistry, I'm afraid."

Faith was still a little suspicious that Michael was only putting on a good face.

"Are you *sure* there's a new woman in your picture, or are you just trying to calm old Faith down?"

"Oh, yes, I'm sure," he said, then got up and called into the living room. "Rita! Can you come in for a minute and meet an old friend?"

A female voice wafted in. "Of course. Just a minute."

Michael turned to Faith. "We grade papers together in the study at night. Rita teaches at Greenleaf High. Spanish. Maybe you can have her run you through a few verbs," he joked.

"Don't you dare tell her I'm flunking Spanish," Faith pleaded. "She'll think I'm a dope."

He put a finger to his lips to show they were sealed. And then a tall, willowy young woman with feathery brown hair came into the kitchen.

"Hi, I'm Rita Kenner," she said, and sat down, and proceeded to, without even trying, both charm Faith and convince her that she was a wonderful person for Michael to be involved with.

After another cup of cocoa and a couple of hours of talk (in which Michael alluded to his and Rita's forthcoming engagement and Faith, tactfully, did not mention Alison's plans to postpone her own wedding), Faith left and walked across campus toward Baker House, full of new thoughts.

When she got to 409, Maggie and Dee's room, the lights were out. She waited until her eyes adjusted to the dark and then found Dana wrapped in an old comforter in the corner. Faith knelt down beside her and whispered, "Are you asleep?"

"No," came a whisper back. "I'm too worried about Alison. How's Michael?"

"In love."

"Oh, I know," Dana said, thinking Faith meant he was still in love with Alison. Faith set her straight.

"The object of his affections is a blond Greenleaf High Spanish teacher named Rita. He's happy as a clam, and sends Alison his best wishes."

"And here we were, so smugly sure Alison and Michael were right for each other. Well, it looks like they're stubbornly refusing to stick to our plan for their lives," Dana said.

The two of them laughed at themselves. Faith stretched out on the floor on her side, at right angles to Dana, taking over a corner of her pillow. They talked like this in the dark while the others slept.

"Faith, I've been lying here thinking for an hour. Even before this news about Michael, I was thinking that we might be barking up the wrong tree here. I mean Jane did have a point. David must love Alison or he wouldn't be going to all this trouble to get her and us to forgive him. It can't be just pride. If that were the case, he could just walk away from the whole mess and say Alison's too demanding and we're too meddlesome. No, I think he's better than we've been giving him credit for."

"I think so, too," Faith said, yawning. "I think he's just new to us. We know Michael and we don't know David, and so we made David into the bad guy. And hyped poor Alison's nerves to the breaking point. I'm surprised her hair's not standing on end by now."

"We've got to do something to get things back on the right course," Dana said.

Faith, who was nearly asleep, said blurrily, "I went to see Michael. It's your turn this time. Go get her, Dana. Talk Alison into unpostponing her wedding." And with that, she rolled over onto her other side, pulling Dana's blanket along with her.

"Okay, okay," Dana said, laughing a little as she sat up.

"Put her cold feet in a warm bath," Faith said, then sank into the deep, even breathing of sleep.

Dana got up stealthily and crept out of the room like a cat.

CHAPTER SIXTEEN

When Dana slipped out of 409 into the hallway, she was a little surprised to see someone else out there so late at night. Another girl, also heading in the direction of the back stairs. In the dim, nightlighted corridor, Dana couldn't tell who it was, only that she was wearing a blue robe and seemed to be in a hurry, moving fast toward the EXIT sign, where she disappeared through the door.

When Dana got to the same door, she pushed it open and headed up, listening to the other girl's footfalls. Thwap, thwap, thwap. Whoever she was, she was wearing shower sandals.

And then there was silence. The girl had reached the top floor and gone through the doorway. She must be going to The Penthouse. Alison's apartment and a large storage room were all there was up there. And so when

Dana pushed open the door herself, she wasn't surprised to find the other girl standing outside Alison's door. She *was* surprised, though, to see that the girl was Toby.

Running into each other like this made both of them awkward.

"Hi," Dana said shyly. "Fancy meeting you here."

"Yeah," Toby said.

"Looks like we both got the same idea at the same time," Dana said.

Toby shook her head.

"Oh, I doubt it's the *same* idea. I mean, I assume you're here because you don't want her to marry David. I'm here because I think she should." She stopped and thought for a moment. "You're not going to beat me up, are you? You were awful stern-sounding about us not coming up here tonight to do any meddling."

"No," Dana said, laughing. "Did I really sound that severe? My bark is much worse than my bite. Actually, I have no bite at all. And besides, I've come over to your side. I came up to try and persuade Alison to get this wedding show back on the road and marry David."

"Oh, great!" Toby sighed. "An ally." And then she stopped to think what odd allies they were. She had no idea what had gone on between Dana and Randy tonight. Maybe she

was standing in this dark hallway with someone who was about to steal away with her boyfriend. Well, her almost-boyfriend.

In the silence surrounding Toby's thoughts,
Dana got a rough idea what those thoughts
were, and began to feel odder about being
here together than Toby did. Over this weekend, she had really come to like Toby. She
respected her honesty and selflessness. It didn't
surprise her that, of all the other girls, Toby
was the one who cared enough about Alison's
dilemma to lose sleep over it and come up
here.

Dana knew Toby was probably wondering
what had happened with Randy. And she
wished she could wipe the worry off Toby's
face by telling her everything was okay, that
she was flying back to Hawaii on Sunday, and
wouldn't give Randy another thought. But
she couldn't say that. And so it seemed better
to stay off the subject entirely, to keep the
focus on Alison.

"Do you want to go in together?" Dana
asked. "As a team?"

"Maybe we're too late," Toby said. "Maybe
she's asleep."

Dana put a finger to her lips and pressed an
ear to the door. After a moment, she backed
off and said, "Nope. It's okay. She's in there
brooding."

"How can you *hear* brooding?" Toby asked

impishly. "What kind of sound does brooding make?"

"It makes the sound of Billie Holliday records. Alison always plays the blues when she's down. Come on, let's try to pull her out of her quicksand."

Dana knocked on the door, first quietly, then, when there was no response, sharply. Soft footsteps padded up to the other side of the door.

"Who is it?" Alison said in a shaky voice.

"It's me. Dana. I've got Toby with me. We need to talk to you."

There was a long pause. For a moment, Dana was afraid Alison wasn't going to let them in. But then the door opened and Alison, hair tangled and matted, eyes red and puffy, stood there looking at them. She was wearing the silk slacks and shirt she'd had on at the shower. Now, though, they looked like they'd been slept in for a week.

"Looking good, Alison," Dana teased. "You should definitely go with that hairdo." Teasing was a gamble here. If Alison took offense, this conversation wouldn't even get off the ground. But it *did* work. Alison's lips broadened into a smile and she reached out to pinch Dana's cheek.

"That's right," she replied, "kick me when I'm down. That's what friends are for."

"You going to invite us in?" Dana went on,

"Or are we going to have to give our pitch out here like door-to-door salespeople?"

Alison stood aside and waved them in. The place was a mess, with magazines strewn all over, open cans of soda, a nearly empty bag of cookies, a table full of crumpled balls of stationery. Dana guessed these were failed attempts at a letter to David. Billie Holiday was singing something tragic from the stereo against the wall, and Doby the cat was wide-eyed and forlorn-looking on the windowsill. It was clearly the apartment of a woman going through a night of major anguish.

Toby and Dana followed Alison. When she flopped down onto the sofa, they sat in the facing easy chair and rocker.

The phone began ringing. But although it was sitting on the arm of the sofa next to Alison, she made no move to answer it. The girls sat counting the rings. Eight. Nine. Ten. It finally stopped at eighteen.

"Maybe he has something to say," Dana said, and told Alison about his videotape.

"He can be so sweet," Alison said, and seemed about to say something else, but then drifted off into thought. It looked to Dana like she had exhausted herself with trying to think this through a million ways.

"Alison," she said. "Give the guy a break. Next time he calls. . . . How many times *has* he called, by the way?"

She expected Alison to be vague about this, too, and so was surprised when she said, "Eleven."

"Well," Dana went on, "next time it rings, why don't you pick it up and just listen to what he has to say? Just give him a chance to apologize and explain."

"I really like David," Toby said, "and I think you two are great together. Please give him another chance. Letting that phone ring like that is just torturing the poor guy."

"I needed to think. There's been so much noise around this wedding, I was losing touch with my feelings. It got so bad I didn't know whether I even *wanted* to get married."

"Don't you think he might be going through some of the same stuff?" Dana said. "Don't you think that might be what your blow-up was really about?"

Alison considered this.

"You two need to talk to each other," Dana pressed on. "Did you tell him you wanted to postpone the wedding?"

Alison shook her head no.

"And I suppose it's a good thing, too," she added.

"Why?" Dana asked.

"Because I don't think I want to postpone it anymore."

"When did you come to this conclusion?" Toby asked.

"Well, to be honest, I'd nearly decided just before you got here. I'd just realized that I could have unplugged that phone hours ago, that I'd been keeping it on so that even though I wasn't answering, I could hear when he called. So I could, in a weird way, be in touch with him through all this.

"If I need to be in touch with him, even when I'm so furious I can't talk to him, I suppose it must be love. And if I love him as much as I know I do, it's got to be the wedding, not the marriage, that's got me all bent out of shape."

"So I'd just about decided to pick up that phone, and tell him I love him and want to marry him. You know, in all the years I've been here, a lot of girls have come up in the middle of the night, but always with *their* problems. This is the first time anyone's ever come up at midnight to see how I'm doing. I'm really touched."

"Aw," Dana said, a little embarrassed. Then she leaped out of her chair and shouted, "All *right*, Alison! It looks like I'm going to get to wear that maid-of-honor dress after all."

"Is that the only reason you came up here to persuade me?" Alison said, pretending to believe it.

"No," Toby said, "there's also my lucky horseshoe. I really don't have room for it in my locker, and if you didn't get married, I was going to be stuck with it."

"So what are you going to do now, Alison?" Dana said. "Wait for David to call the twelfth time?"

"No. I think I'll call him."

Dana and Toby nodded and Alison nodded back, and then the three of them just sat there for a minute looking at each other. It began to seem as though Alison was waiting for something. Toby was the first to figure out what it was. She slapped her forehead.

"Argh," she said.

"What?" Dana said, still not getting it.

"Are we thick, or what? I do believe Alison, weird person that she is, would rather have this conversation with her boyfriend *without* us around. Can you believe it?"

Dana burst out laughing, and got out of her chair to follow Toby.

"Sorry," she said, backing toward the door as Alison punched the buttons of David's number and said, "David, it's me. I was just wondering if you were doing anything special tomorrow afternoon. Because if you're free, I thought maybe you'd like to get married."

CHAPTER
SEVENTEEN

After having been up so late the night before, Toby slept in on Saturday. She was the last one awake in 407. Andy and Jane were already coming back from late breakfast, when she sat up in bed and peered out through sleepy eyes.

"What time is it?" she asked.

"Around ten-thirty. We thought maybe you were planning to sleep through the wedding."

"You heard that it's back on?" Toby said, putting her legs over the side of the bed, onto the floor.

"Alison was down at breakfast, delirious with happiness. She gave us the news. She gave everybody the news. She practically had a megaphone."

Andy walked over to the windows and sat down on the window seat, pulling her feet up, wrapping her arms around her legs, as she stared bleakly out.

"Still pouring," she said glumly.

"It's raining?" Toby said.

"Cats and dogs," Jane said. "Poor Alison. What a day for a wedding. We'll all look like drowned rats by the time we get over to the chapel. Alison's so happy, though, she doesn't care. She says if she has to, she'll get married in her raincoat. I myself am going to have to go in a paper bag to avoid the tricky problem of having two dates for this event."

"What two dates?" Toby and Andy asked in unison.

Jane told them the whole story, then said, "So you see, I don't know what to do."

"You have to tell Cary there's been a mistake," Toby said. "It's the only honest thing to do."

"But I'd rather *go* with Cary," she pouted.

"Doesn't matter," Andy said. "You made a commitment to Neal and you've got to stick to it. If Matt Dillon called, you'd have to turn him down."

"But Neal's train doesn't leave for an hour. I could tell him I'm not feeling well and I'm skipping the wedding."

Neither Toby nor Andy even dignified this proposition with a reply. They just stared squarely at Jane.

"You're too hard on me," she told them. "I thought friends were there to support you in a crisis."

"Sometimes support is helping someone see

her way clear to doing the right thing," Toby said.

"Well, call it support if you want, but *I* call it abandoning your roommate in a moment of need!" Jane said, then stormed out of the room.

And then, while Toby and Andy were still sitting stunned, looking at the doorway, Jane came back through it, groaned loudly, flopped on her bed, and stuck her feet straight up in the air.

"All *right*," she said with resignation. "You win. I know it's the right thing to do. But I don't want to make this call to Cary, telling him not to come."

"I got brownies in the mail from my folks today," Andy said. "Call Cary and I'll give you one."

"That's pretty cheap psychology," Jane said.

"But you'll do it," Andy encouraged.

"Yes," Jane said, then growled at both of them as she got up and headed down to the pay phones. "I couldn't stand having you two look at me for the rest of my years here as if I were a total rat."

No sooner was she out the door than she popped her head back in to say, "You'd better make that *two* brownies!"

Usually there was a long line at the pay phones, but this morning there were only a couple of girls ahead of Jane, and so she only had to wait a few minutes before dialing the number of Cary Slade's dorm room at Oakley Prep. His roommate answered.

"Hi, Stu," she said. "Cary there?"

"Nope." Stu never used any more words than he had to.

"Do you know where he is?"

"Tuxedo shop."

"What?"

"Tuxedo shop."

"Yes, Stu. I managed to get that. Maybe you could tell me *why* he's at the tuxedo shop." But she'd really already guessed.

"He's picking up some monkey suit he's rented for some dumb wedding."

Jane felt her heart sink.

"I see," she said. "Well, could you have him call me when he gets back?"

"Won't be for a while. After the tux, he's going to the flower shop, and then — "

But Jane had already heard enough.

"Thanks, Stu," she said, and hung up the receiver. She trudged back to 407. As she came into the room, the incoming phone started ringing. Maybe it was Cary! Maybe he hadn't really gotten to the tux shop and the florist yet.

"Hi," Jane said into the phone.

"Hi, yourself." It was Alison. Her voice was all lit up. She sounded like someone on a

commercial who'd discovered a terrific product. "You guys want to help the bride get
ready?" she asked.

"Oh, great!" Jane said. "Of course we do.
We'll be right up!" She'd have to worry about
boy problems later. This was going to be too
much fun. She wasn't going to waste it being
worried.

She hung up, turned to Andy and Toby,
and said, "Come on! We've got to turn Alison
into a bride!"

Dana, Faith, and Shelley were already up in
The Penthouse when the younger girls got
there. Alison didn't seem at all the nervous
bride. Actually, she didn't seem like any kind
of bride. She was wearing her oldest, most
faded jeans, a Virginia Woolf T-shirt, and
tennis shoes with holes in the toes. She'd lost
her good glasses, and so she was wearing her
old ones, with the sidepiece hinged to the
front part with adhesive tape. Her hair was
even more of a mess than it had been the
night before. Andy, Toby, and Jane just stood
for a moment looking at her, wondering how
she was going to be presentable enough to
walk down the aisle in a couple of hours.

She must have seen the alarm in their eyes
as she laughed and said, "Well . . . you can
see why I need all six of you to help me out."

They were all behind Alison marrying
David, but there were still a lot of chafed

feelings among them. Shelley couldn't quite forget the smugly superior attitude Jane had taken toward her from the beginning.

And it would be a while before Jane forgot that hunk of cake. She was a Barrett of the Boston Barretts, a family unaccustomed to getting hunks of chocolate cake pushed in their faces.

Toby wanted to like Dana, but was still wary of her interest in Randy. Was it sincere? Did it threaten her?

Faith felt she had begun making real gestures of friendship toward Andy, but wasn't sure Andy was accepting them.

But whatever their differences, all of them, without saying so much as a word to each other about it, had decided to drop them for today and get along for the sake of Alison having the world's most perfect wedding.

They started by surveying the raw material for their make-over.

"Luckily you're naturally beautiful, Alison," Dana said. "All we have to do is put you into Bridal Mode." She turned to the others and said, "We've got to be like those little mice and birds who got Cinderella ready for the ball. And we've got to get going." She turned back to Alison and told her, "First we'll run you a bubble bath, then we'll wash and style your hair. I will personally work you over with my makeup collection *extraordinaire*."

Everyone contributed their talents to this enterprise. Jane brought up her special herbal shampoo and washed Alison's chestnut hair. Shelley, who was the best stylist among them, used hot rollers to soften the hair into a cascade of curls.

As promised, Dana served as makeup artist, giving Alison just enough color to approximate a light spring tan, then highlighted her cheeks with blush. She did Alison's eyes with two shades of shadow, blue and silver, a fine line of black liner, and two coats of mascara to double Alison's fine lashes. For lipstick, she used a soft pink with gloss over it.

"There," she said, stepping back so the others could see what she'd done.

"Looking good, Alison," said Toby, who had spent the past half-hour combing The Penthouse to find Alison's good pair of glasses. Now, she pulled them from behind her back, and exchanged them for the adhesive-taped pair she pulled off Alison's nose.

Alison smiled and squeezed Toby's hand in thanks. Then she peered into the mirror that Faith had handed her and took her first look at the new her.

"Oh, my," she said, clearly stunned. "This is such a gorgeous version of me. Are you sure it *is* me?"

"All that's missing is your dress and veil," Andy said, and then, looking over at the long

box on the sofa, asked Alison, "Can we try the
veil on! Oh, please?!"

Alison laughed, and said, "Sure. Go get it."

Andy came out holding the veil as if it were
made of spider's web. She put it on and rushed
to the long mirror on the door of Alison's old
pine armoire and stood gazing at herself. After
a while, Shelley came up and did the same.
Each of them took a turn, each girl having the
same fantasy as she looked at her own reflec-
tion — imagining herself as a bride.

Then they all wanted to see Alison's wedding gown.

"Will you try it on for us? Dana, too?" Alison had both the bride's and maid of honor's
dresses in garment bags in the closet, but no
one had seen them except Dana, who'd had
hers fitted when she arrived.

"Tell you what," Alison said. "Why don't
you all get yourselves dressed up and ready
and come back here. Then Dana and I will
model for you. And hurry up," she added,
looking at her huge Mickey Mouse watch.
"The wedding's supposed to start in an hour
and we still have to get through this rain over
to the chapel." Faith, noticing the watch,
came back and took it off Alison's wrist, lest
she absentmindedly wear it down the aisle.

When the girls reassembled half an hour later
they were a rainbow of colors — from Toby's

beige outfit. To Andy's rust-colored wool dress. To Shelley's red silk dress (which looked great with her blond hair). To Faith's unstructured gray linen jacket and baggy pleated pants. To Jane's blue tweed blazer and velvet skirt with a peach silk shirt.

Alison and Dana had dressed in the bedroom and waited to make their grand entrance until the others were all ready. Both dresses had come from Alison's Irish family. Her bridal gown had been worn by her great grandmother at *her* wedding. Dana's dress had been worn on stage by one of Alison's great aunts who sang opera. The two of them emerged from the bedroom as they would coming down the aisle . . . Dana first, followed by the bride.

For a joke, they made this walk using the traditional halt-step.

"Ohhh, you both look so wonderful!" Shelley said, and she said it for all of them because they really *did* look wonderful. Dana's dress was rose-colored taffeta with cream lace inserts and tiny seed pearls at the bodice. Alison's floor-length white dress had puffed shoulders and a scalloped neckline. The long sleeves were old lace, as was the deep hem. Both of them were wearing heels and gloves to match their dresses.

"This has a train, too," Alison said. "I just didn't want to put that on until the last minute. The veil, either. Once I get all that on, I'm not going to want to walk around much. I don't wear heels all that often, not to mention floor-length dresses. The bottom line for me is that I'd like to get through this event without tripping and falling flat on my face. I don't want everyone remembering me until my dying day as 'The Bride Who Tripped.' "

There was a knock on the door. Alison turned, startled.

"Come in."

Everyone was surprised to see Patrice Allardyce standing in the doorway. She was clearly all ready for the wedding in a navy suit and a wide, picture brim hat.

She cleared her throat. She was so used to making announcements and pronouncements, that she tended to begin all conversations this way.

"I don't want to disturb you all," she said, and then went on before anyone could indicate that she was or wasn't a disturbance. "But I heard that you girls followed my favorite old bridal verse when you got Alison her gifts."

"Yes," Alison said, smiling. "It was a great idea. I have my camisole, my something old, on underneath. And if I didn't think it would look a little weird, I'd go down that aisle holding my horseshoe and toaster, and wearing my flippers."

"Well," Ms. Allardyce went on, "the thing of it is that there's another bit to the rhyme. It's:

> *Something old,*
> *Something new,*
> *Something borrowed,*
> *Something blue.*
> *And a sixpence in her shoe."*

"What's a sixpence?" Toby asked.

"Why, it's an old English coin, of course," Ms. Allardyce said.

"But where would we get one at this last minute?" Faith wondered.

Ms. Allardyce smiled.

"That's why I'm here," she said and produced a shiny coin from the pocket of her suit jacket. "I polished it up a bit, Alison. Now slip it in your shoe for good luck."

"Why, thank you, Patrice. It's nice to know you were thinking about me."

"Oh, goodness, I've had to think about you a lot lately what with all the candidates I've had to interview for your post. But I think I may have found just the right one to take your place."

"Oh?" Alison said distractedly. She was busy giving herself a last-minute inspection in the mirror. "What school is she at now?"

"Well, her career thus far hasn't been exactly in education. Not in the usual sense, anyway. She's with the circus, actually. She has an act for which she trains wild animals. She thinks she can apply a lot of the same methods to governing Canby Hall girls."

Everyone stood silently aghast at this, until they saw the smile cracking Ms. Allardyce's set lips. And then they all realized that she was kidding. Which was even more amazing — Patrice Allardyce kidding! When they laughed, they were really laughing more at this than at her joke.

When the laughter died down, Alison said, "Well, I suppose we'd better head over to the chapel."

Then she turned to see how hard the rain was coming down. She was, along with the rest of them, astonished. The driving rain had been replaced by a brilliant sun. When they all got down onto the front lawn of Baker and looked up in the sky, they had their breath taken away.

"A double rainbow," Toby said. "You don't see many of those. Not even if you look up at the sky all the time. It's a great sign!" She turned to Alison. "Don't worry about tripping anymore. Today's going to be charmed for you!"

CHAPTER EIGHTEEN

Alison and the girls got over to the chapel with about fifteen minutes to spare before the wedding was scheduled to begin. In that quarter hour of waiting in the cloakroom at the back of the chapel, Alison went from ecstasy to nervous collapse. The cause was an acute absence of groom. David was nowhere to be found.

"He's not going to show up," Alison moaned with the voice of doom, as she peered out the cloakroom doorway and watched the ushers seating the growing number of guests: Canby Hall girls and faculty, old friends and relatives. David's parents were already there, in the front row on the groom's side.

"It looks like I'm going to have a full house to witness my humiliation," Alison added.

"Quit talking like that. He's on his way," Jane said, trying to sound reassuring. She was scanning the crowd for her own purposes.

Sure enough, there were both Neal and Cary. And it looked like they had run into each other on the way in. They were sitting together, talking. Probably wondering why they were *both* at this wedding. Although each of them knew about the other's presence in Jane's life, she was pretty sure they'd probably rather not be on the *same* date with her. How ironic, she thought, that Alison's dilemma this morning was one too few grooms while hers was one too many boyfriends.

Now Andy was trying to reassure Alison from another angle.

"Look. You talked to him just this morning," she said. "So you know everything's all right." These words came out a little garbled due to the several hairpins she had clenched in her teeth. She was trying to get Alison's veil on straight.

"No," Alison said.

"No what?" Andy said.

"No, I didn't talk with him today. You know the old superstition."

"But that's about not *seeing* the groom before the wedding," said Jane, who was the expert in traditions. "Just talking on the phone wouldn't count."

"We weren't sure," Alison said. "And this wedding has caused so much trouble already . . . well, we didn't want to push our luck."

The door of the cloakroom pushed open. They all looked up expectantly, thinking it might be David. But it was another man, this one with dark good looks: thick black hair, deep brown eyes, a strong jaw, and teeth out of a toothpaste ad.

"Oh, Vince," Alison said, exhaling with relief. "You guys finally got here." And then the others recognized him as Vince Santini, *Nighttime News* sportscaster and David's best friend. And today, his best man. But he didn't seem to understand what Alison was talking about. She tried again.

"You *did* come up with David, didn't you?"

Vince shook his head. "No, he said he needed his car afterward to go off with you. I have to head straight back to Boston tonight so I drove up by myself. Why? Isn't he here yet?"

The silence in the room gave him his answer.

"Well, don't worry. He will be. David loves weddings. Wouldn't miss one for the world. Says weddings are the only place where you can both get free champagne *and* do the Mexican Hat Dance with your aunt."

But none of Vince's kidding around had any noticeable effect. Alison, and now the girls, were beginning to get truly worried. It was now nearly quarter past three.

"Jilted at the altar," Alison moaned.

"You're not jilted," Vince consoled her. "And you're not at the altar. You're only slightly detained in the cloakroom."

The door pushed open again. This time it was Mr. and Mrs. Cavanaugh, Alison's parents.

"Ohhh, don't you look lovely in grandmother's dress," Mrs. Cavanaugh said, first hugging her daughter, then holding her at arms' length to get a better look. And then she saw Dana and gushed again. "And you, Dana, in Aunt Gertrude's opera dress! Oh, my. And Vince, I don't think I've ever seen you so dressed up. You ought to wear a tux more often. And all you girls look so pretty in these outfits." Then she spun around and asked, "Now where's that handsome groom?"

"Oh," Alison said, then couldn't think of anything more to say.

"On his way," Vince said in his most confident, sportscasting voice. "He'll be here any minute now."

"But shhh," Jane cautioned, putting a finger to her lips, "you know it's bad luck for the parents of the bride to talk about the groom before the wedding."

"Never heard that one," Alison's father mused.

"Oh, it's a big superstition in Boston," Jane lied, knowing Alison's parents were from Amherst.

"Well, come on, Frank," Mrs. Cavanaugh said. "Superstitions aside, I want to get out there and sit in that first row so I can turn and look when you bring our little Bunny down the aisle."

All the girls exchanged looks around an embarrassed Alison and mouthed the word "bunny" at each other. They all knew that you found out the funniest stuff about friends when their parents came around.

When Vince had taken Mr. and Mrs. Cavanaugh out, Alison sighed loudly.

"Oh, Jane, you were great with that instant 'tradition.' And if anyone in this room so much as mentions the word 'bunny,' I will go into full-scale hysteria. I'm on the edge already so it wouldn't take much. What time is it now, by the way?" she asked nervously, looking at her wrist, which was now watchless.

"About twenty-five after," said Toby, who was nearly incapable of telling a lie, or even fudging the truth a little. Andy gave her a swift elbow in the ribs, but it was too late.

"He's simply not coming," Alison said matter-of-factly, her hands belying her true emotions, though, as she twisted her antique lace handkerchief as if she were wringing it out. "Someone should go out and inform the guests. Tell them to go home. The show has been canceled."

"Come on, Alison," Dana said, draping a comforting arm over Alison's shoulders. "Don't sink into the depths of despair just yet. I'll go call David's apartment in Boston. Make sure he didn't oversleep or something."

But this proved futile. When Dana returned from the pay phone, it was three-thirty-five and she had only gotten his answering tape.

"So at least it looks like he hasn't moved out of town," she joked, but it was hollow humor.

It was about then that Father Colligan, in his white and gold vestments, opened the door and stuck his head in. The bleating strains of the chapel organ wafted in behind him.

"Ladies, I think we're ready now, so if you'd like to begin," he said tactfully.

Alison smiled feebly and said, "Well, we seem to be missing a small detail . . . the groom."

"Oh," Father Colligan said with a hearty joviality, "happens all the time. They get a slightly chilled set of feet. But they usually warm up in the end. Of course, some never do show," he mused unhelpfully. "I'll tell Mrs. Sinkowski to play a medley of wedding favorites to keep the crowd lulled. Give him a few more minutes. I'm sure he'll turn up. I'm sure you won't wind up like poor Rosie Forrester. She got all the way to the altar before she realized there was no one waiting there for her. Gave her quite a bad moment there. People still mention it whenever they talk about her."

"Uh, Father . . ." Faith said, gently leading him out of the room.

By three-forty, Alison told the girls to call the men in the white coats to take her away — her nerves were completely shot.

At three forty-two, though, Toby heard something. Within the next minute, the others began to hear it, too. Hard, fast hoof-beats. Jane rushed to the small window of the cloakroom and pulled back the heavy velvet curtains. The others crowded behind her trying to get a glimpse. At first all they could see was that a horse was approaching very fast. Then they could see that there were two riders — both blond, both male. Finally, they could see that the front one was Randy, in jeans and a red shirt and a bandanna head-band. Behind him, hanging on for dear life, and dressed in a pearl-gray tuxedo, was David!

The cloakroom went up for grabs, with all the girls, along with Alison, screaming and shouting and jumping up and down. They ran outside onto the lawn of the chapel just in time to be there as Randy brought his horse up short and gave David a hand down off the horse.

"Found this guy out on the old highway with a dead sports car. I told him he ought to trade it in for a horse. *Their* carburetors never break down. Anyway, I figured you might be wanting him around for this wedding . . . a mere formality, I know, but still. . . ."

David went straight for Alison, and swept her up in a kiss.

"But David," she said, "what about superstition?"

"I don't give a hoot about superstitions," he said, took both her hands in his, and said seriously, "I'm sorry if I gave you any anxious moments."

"Anxious moments?" Alison said blithely. "Oh, no. Actually, we'd gotten up a game of hearts in the cloakroom, and your being a little late gave us a chance to finish. I was winning, so I was kind of hoping you'd take your time."

"Well, in that case, maybe Randy and I should've stopped for breakfast. I don't mean to rush you."

Alison replied by grabbing David's ear and tugging him into the chapel. David shouted over his shoulder at Randy. "Hey, you've got to stay for this. You've got to be our guest of honor."

Then he turned to Alison and said, "I'll go up to the front of the chapel now and meet with Vince. But I'll be waiting for you there, watching every step you take toward me."

Alison's father was waiting in the chapel vestibule, ready to take his daughter down the aisle. They stood at the back while the girls filed into the chapel. Andy, Jane, and Shelley sat in the second pew, right behind Mrs. Cavanaugh. Toby, pulling a reluctant Randy by the hand, followed them. Faith, who'd offered to serve as wedding photographer, was here, there, and everywhere with her camera.

Mrs. Sinkowski stopped her warm-up repertoire, murky tunes that sounded like the organ was underwater, and, after a theatrical pause, her hands poised high above the keyboard, she lurched into "Here Comes the Bride." Everyone in the chapel turned to see Dana, holding a bouquet of roses to match her gown, leading the march down the aisle, down which the ushers had unrolled a white bridal runner. There were also red roses on the simple pine altar, and in sconces at the end of each of the white-painted pews. A floral scent filled the room.

Behind Dana, Mr. Cavanaugh beamed as he held his daughter's hand on his arm and escorted her to the altar, where David and Vince were waiting side by side in tuxedos with a 1930's cut, and tiny wing collars on the shirts. Vince's tux was black while David's was gray, but they each wore a rose in their lapel to match the bouquets that Alison and Dana were carrying.

Alison was, even more than most brides, radiant. Bathed in the brilliant colors of sunlight streaming through the stained glass windows of the chapel, she was enveloped in a special glow. And ironically, the tears she'd been crying in the cloakroom had only heightened the color in her cheeks and left her eyes bright and clear. The past hour had used up all her reserves of nervousness, leaving her to sail through the wedding on a cloud of calm.

When Alison got to the front of the chapel, her father stepped aside and David took her arm the rest of the way, until they were standing in front of Father Colligan, with Dana and Vince behind them.

The ceremony was brief. Father Colligan led Alison and David through their vows . . .

> *. . . for richer, for poorer,*
> *in sickness and in health,*
> *from this day forward,*
> *as long as we both shall live.*

Then he blessed the rings, matching narrow gold bands, which they slipped on each other's fingers . . .

> *. . . with this ring, I thee wed.*

And finally, he pronounced them man and wife. And then he pronounced them woman and husband, an addition to the ceremony written in by Alison, who was an ardent feminist.

And when David lifted Alison's veil and leaned in to kiss the bride, there wasn't a dry eye among Dana, Shelley, Andy, Toby, and Jane. Faith, who was crouched off to the side of the altar rail to get a picture of the kiss, had to put her camera down for a moment and wipe her tears away before she could go on. Even the always-cool and aloof Patrice Allardyce was sniffling a little.

And then Mrs. Sinkowski pumped the foot pedals of the old organ and crashed into the resounding chords of the wedding march, as David and Alison bounded back up the aisle and out of the chapel, followed by Dana, who was pleasantly surprised to find her hand taken by Vince on the way out. She looked up and caught his smile. Was he interested in her, she wondered, or just doing his duty as best man, pairing up with the maid of honor? Hmmm.

Dana's absorption at the moment with Vince, and with the duties of a maid of honor — signing the marriage certificate, posing for photos — left Toby with Randy all to herself. They walked through the sun-dappled afternoon into the churchyard, where he'd tethered his horse. He told her all about his rescue of David.

"Wish I'd been there to see it," she said.

"Oh, you probably would've just stole my thunder with some Annie Oakley move," he teased. "You wouldn't have even stopped for David, just picked him up by his collar as you rode by. Back-flipped him into the saddle, then galloped up the aisle, and deposited him at the altar."

"Aw, come on," she said, but she was smiling.

"Well, maybe your style would've been slightly cramped by that outfit."

"You don't like it?" she said.

"I like it very much," he admitted. "It makes you look dressed up without looking like you're working too hard at it."

"Oh," Toby said, a little disappointed at this practical assessment.

"It also makes you look even prettier than usual."

"Oh," she said again, but it was a different kind of "oh."

On the stone steps of the chapel, Faith took formal pictures of the wedding party, along with a gag photo featuring all of them wearing Groucho nose-and-glasses masks, which she'd brought along for fun. Off to the side, Jane was trying to get out of the mess she'd gotten herself into with Cary and Neal.

In her head, she had gone through all the possible lies, and ultimately decided they wouldn't buy any of them. So she was more or less forced to tell the truth. But once forced, she kind of forgot that she'd been forced and started thinking she ought to get points for her honesty, that both guys really ought to let her off the hook, have a laugh about it, go on to the reception together.

Unfortunately, neither of them shared this point of view. They were both furious with her.

"How could you invite us both to this as your date?" asked Neal, who had come all dressed up in a charcoal pinstripe suit and a burgundy bow tie.

"I even rented this," Cary said, gesturing to indicate the powder-blue dinner jacket with silver lapels that he was wearing with jeans and a black T-shirt, his interpretation of "formal."

"Oh, please, give me a break, will you?" she begged them. "I know I didn't handle this well, but the harm's done now. We're all here and that's that. I don't see that there's anything to be done about it."

The two guys looked at each other and, speaking for both of them, Neal said, "Oh, we've thought of something to do about it."

And they left. Just like that, without another word. And they took off at a brisk lope so that Jane, in her heels, couldn't catch up with them. And she didn't want to shout and get the attention of the entire wedding crowd. So all she could do was stand there and watch helplessly as they disappeared into the distance.

As she was doing this, Andy came up behind her and kiddingly said, "How's the double date going?"

Jane turned, put a hand on Andy's shoulder, and said, "I think it just got up and went."

CHAPTER NINETEEN

The reception was a dinner dance in the Hunt Room of the Greenleaf Inn. The inn was a landmark in town, dating back to the 1700's. It was said that George Washington had spent a night there, and that behind the walls were secret passages. It was a place filled with historic glamour, perfect for a traditional bride like Alison.

The dinner was elegant, served buffet-style on a long table covered with ivory linen and with food that was at the opposite end of the spectrum from Baker House fare: prime rib, Caesar salad, and broccoli with hollandaise sauce.

"Do you think it would be tacky if we asked for doggie bags?" Andy kidded Jane, who had her plate heaped high and wasn't even halfway to the end of the buffet.

Faith came up behind them, clicked a picture, and said, "I do love prime rib, but philosophically speaking, is it really *ribs*?!"

She was teasing Andy, whose family owned a restaurant in Chicago that specialized in barbecued ribs, a food that Andy felt only blacks really knew how to cook.

Andy smiled, and whispered, "No way. But I'm not going to criticize. The only ribs I've had since I got to Canby Hall are the Baker House version of Oriental sweet and sour ribs. Dee says they make the sauce with pancake syrup and vinegar. So these prime ribs are prime with me. The whole dinner looks great. I wonder if I could find someone rich who'd bring me here for dinner every night?"

"What about your boyfriend over there?" Faith said, pointing at Matt, who had already filled his plate and was sitting down talking with Toby and Randy.

Andy shook her head. "Poor as a church-mouse."

"But cute," Faith said, pointing her camera in his direction and snapping a photo.

"You think so?" Andy said, trying to sound cool, but secretly pleased that Faith liked him. "I guess I do, too."

"Give me a smile, girl," Faith said, taking a close-up of Andy.

"What do you want a picture of me for?" Andy said.

"Oh, I'm doing a photo essay on bratty girls who give their elders no respect."

"I give you plenty of respect," Andy retorted. "I just don't let you see it. I don't want you to get any more impressed with yourself than you already are."

In retaliation, Faith made a sudden move, as if she were going to push Andy's overloaded dinner plate from beneath and tip it over.

"Now you get out of there!" Andy said, laughing. "Be nice to me and I might let you dance with my cute date."

"*That's* a deal!" Faith said. "Now, have either of you seen Dana? I want to get a picture of her, too."

Jane looked around and said, "Oh, there she is, in the living room, talking with Vince."

Dana and Vince had been talking for nearly an hour now, sitting on the chintz-covered sofa in front of the fireplace, which had a low, crackling fire going in it. They were talking about their mutually favorite place on earth — Manhattan. They both came from there and hoped to eventually get back. As it turned out, Dana's mother and Vince's parents lived within two blocks of each other. So they had a lot of common memories and favorite spots.

"What about Zabar's?" Dana asked him now. "Did you ever go there? Isn't it the greatest deli?"

"But for great sandwiches, you've got to go to the Stage Deli," he countered.

"Oh, there are moments up here when I'd give anything for a really good corned beef sandwich," she sighed.

And then they were off on great movie houses. And then the best places to get funky clothes cheap. And then they tried to top each other with knowing the weirdest haircutting places.

For a moment, Dana got a little nervous. She thought, I really ought to go over and talk with Randy. But then she looked around the Room and saw that he seemed to be happily eating dinner with Toby, so she went back to talking with Vince.

"And what about that place down in Soho that sells bagels and sportswear?!"

When Jane finished dinner, she stayed on at the table, sipping coffee and watching Alison and David cut the wedding cake, leaning over it to kiss each other. She watched the band set up for the after-dinner dancing. All of a sudden she felt a chill. She looked behind her to see that one of the French doors had opened. And coming through it was Cary Slade.

"What are you doing here?" she said, truly surprised. She knew she had behaved weakly this afternoon, letting the mix-up happen. She knew that he and Neal had had a right to stomp off like they did. She had even come to accept that having no date for the wedding was a fitting punishment.

He pulled up a chair and sat down next to her. In spite of it being fairly cold outside, he wasn't wearing a coat over his wild tux jacket. He took her hands in his.

"For warmth," he explained.

"Oh, that's all?" she teased.

"Well, I *am* still pretty mad at you," he said.

"Then why are you here?"

"Well, I was walking Neal to the train depot and I told him we were cutting off our nose to spite our face. We walk out on you and you get to stay at the wedding and have all the fun. That didn't seem fair."

"So?" she said, looking around. "Is he here with you?"

"No. I couldn't talk him into coming back. He said it would violate his code of ethics. He expects you to make a formal apology, in writing, notarized, delivered by bonded messenger. And then he'll decide if he'll ever speak to you again."

"He didn't say that?"

"No." Cary shook his head. "He *was* hurt, though. I think you ought to give him a call later tonight when he gets back to Boston. Tell him you're really sorry. Offer to take him out for dinner the next weekend you're home."

"Hey, wait a minute!" Jane said, laughing. "Why are you giving me such good advice on my relationship with my other boyfriend?

How come you're so generous with your counseling?"

"Because, my darling Jane, when all is said and done, there's no way Cornelius Worthington III, your Neal, will be able to win out against the charms of the rock and roll madman, Cary Slade. I can afford to be generous in the meantime."

"Why, you conceited little . . ." she said, pulling back her hand into a fist, which Cary grabbed.

"Now, now. Debutantes don't punch," he kidded.

"Well, tell me this," she said. "How come you've forgiven me?"

"Who's forgiven you?" he said. "I just came to listen to the band. I hear they're terrific," he said sarcastically. "They've got a great image — those matching suits — and I like their name. The Treble Clefs."

"I heard these guys get a lot of work playing at weddings and parties. They probably make a ton of money. I don't think you ought to be so critical. The only time Ambulance ever got paid was when you played the opening of that sub shop and the owner gave you free sandwiches."

"Ouch," he said, pretending to wince. "You really know how to hurt a guy."

By now the band had warmed up and was launching into its first number, an elevator music version of "Proud Mary."

"Oh, no!" Cary groaned. "They're going to ruin rock and roll! Can't someone put them under house arrest?"

But no one else seemed to mind that they were awful. A party mood was percolating, and dancing was one of everyone's favorite ways to party. First out onto the floor were Shelley, Faith, and Andy, who was very possibly the best dancer, ballet or disco, at Canby Hall. Matt joined them, then Dana and Vince, who found they danced with the same sort of style. Then the bride and groom joined in.

Toby stood to the side of the dance floor with Randy, who'd gone home between the wedding and reception and changed into a navy suit with a pale pink shirt and tie. She didn't think she'd ever seen him look more wonderful. Neither of them had mentioned Dana tonight. She hadn't come by to talk with him, though, and Toby couldn't help wondering how Randy felt, watching her be completely captivated by Vince.

"Do you do this kind of dancing?" she asked him.

"Do you?" he asked her.

They both shook their heads no, and then watched everyone else for a while more. The Treble Clefs were now murdering the Stones' "Tumbling Dice."

"Doesn't look all that hard," Randy speculated.

"Just a lot of hopping around," was Toby's analysis.

"You know," he said to her. "If we can get huge wild horses to move just the way we want them to, we ought to be able to get our feet under control on a dance floor."

"You're right," she said, and they tentatively edged out onto the polished wood, and began moving around each other in a way that was kind of like dancing. After a while of this, they dropped their frowns of concentration and smiled at each other.

"What are Toby and Randy doing over there?" Cary said, still sitting next to Jane at the end of their table. He'd gotten a plate of food from the buffet and was just finishing his dinner.

"I think they're teaching themselves to dance," Jane said. "You know, people who are too timid to get out on the floor shouldn't throw stones at people who actually *dance*."

"I'm not timid. I just don't have the time right now. I have to go call the Rolling Stones' lawyer and get him to sue this band for what they're doing to this song."

"Come on," Jane said, standing up and pulling Cary away from the last of his prime rib, out onto the floor. "Enough of your sarcasm and critiques. Get out here and make a fool of yourself like everyone else!"

* * *

Later, when Toby went into the ladies' room, she found Dana there, brushing the long brown hair Toby remembered envying the first time they met.

"Just the person I want to talk to," Dana said, seeing Toby in the mirror.

"About our mutual friend," Toby guessed, hiking herself up on the sink next to where Dana was standing.

"Mmmhmm. I've been thinking a lot about him tonight."

"You could've fooled me."

"No, really. When he and I got together last night, it was like old times. This whole weekend has been so nostalgic. But I think nostalgia can trip you up sometimes. You only remember the good parts. Or a simpler time looks better than the complicated life you have now, but it's just that you're forgetting all the complications back then.

"I told Randy I'd think about him and me. As a possibility. And last night it really *did* seem like a possibility. But as soon as I got back to the dorm and started thinking about my ambitions to be a writer and a marathon runner. . . . And then today, meeting Vince . . . well, he's so interested in so many of the things I am. . . ."

"So now you're interested in Vince?" Toby said.

"Not Vince himself exactly, although he *is* pretty cute, but guys *like* Vince. Randy is one of the most wonderful people I've ever met. I guess I don't have to tell you that. But I don't know if we'd have enough to talk about for fifty years, or even five years. We had that problem when I was here, and since then I've only become more like me and he's become more like himself. I guess what I'm saying is that, realistically, it probably wouldn't work out."

Dana looked at Toby in the mirror, then turned and looked her squarely in the eyes.

"I guess I am relieved," Toby said. "But I can't say why exactly. I mean, it's not as though I'm going to ride off into the sunset with him. He's still twenty and I'm still fifteen and we're still just friends. But even though we don't have any real present together, I'm sort of glad to hear you aren't going to be tying up his future."

Dana smiled at Toby's directness.

"You know, I really wish you'd been at Canby Hall in my day," she said. "I've a feeling we would've been good friends."

Toby smiled, then jumped off the sink and gave Dana a little push.

"Now," she said. "Go tell *him* what you told me."

Out on the dance floor, everyone was getting into the act. During one of the slow numbers, Dana and Randy danced a sort of "no hard feelings" dance. A waltz brought Mr. and Mrs.

Cavanaugh out onto the floor, along with David's parents. And then they all stayed on to polka. By far the most amazing couple for this number, "Roll Out the Barrel," was Cary Slade and Patrice Allardyce. Everyone stopped and blinked as they polka-ed by.

"I told you," David said to Vince. "Weddings are wild." And then to Alison, "I'm glad I finally showed up for this one."

She hitched up her long skirt a little to give him a mock kick in the shins.

"Ouch," he said, pantomiming pain, then, "Hey, isn't it about time we got ready to leave?"

"Where are you two going?" Dana asked. "Or is it a secret?"

"Well, since Patrice gave me a couple of days off as a wedding present, I think we're going to drive to Niagara Falls."

"Niagara Falls!" Dana said, laughing.

"Hey. What can I say? Weddings bring out my corny side," Alison said, as David grabbed her hand and they ran up the stairs together. When they had changed into casual clothes, David came downstairs, but Alison stood at the top and shouted down, "All my girls, gather round. I'm going to toss my bouquet."

"What's that about?" Toby asked Dana.

"Whoever catches the bouquet is supposed to be the next one to get married," Dana explained. "Come on. It'll be fun."

And so they all clustered at the foot of the stairs, their hands in the air expectantly as Alison turned her back to them and tossed the cluster of roses over her shoulder.

Shelley saw it coming straight at her. She just opened her hands and there it was. She stared for a moment, looking at the flowers in astonishment.

Then Jane, standing next to her, asked, "Do you know who it'll be?" she asked. "Who you'll marry?"

Shelley shook her head. "But when I *do* get married, I'm going to have a wedding just like this."

"Except if you have it back in Iowa, you'll have to hold the reception in a barn, won't you?"

Shelley started to get furious, then noticed the twinkle in Jane's eye.

"I probably shouldn't kid around with you," Jane said. "I'm likely to get a piece of wedding cake smashed in my face."

"Oh. I'm sorry about that. I don't know what came over me."

"Well, I probably provoked you a bit this week," Jane admitted. "I'm not really as much of a snob as I come off sometimes."

"You just think Boston's the center of the universe," Shelley said.

"You mean it isn't?" Jane responded, and they both had to laugh. Then Andy and Faith came up with a large paper bag between them.

"Come on and help us out," Faith murmured, then winked to show them skulduggery was afoot.

"We're going to send the bride and groom off in style."

The bag was full of tin cans, which they tied, along with a JUST MARRIED sign, to the rear bumper of Alison's old Chevy, the wedding car now that David's was out of commission. And then, as everyone came out onto the front steps of the inn, they furtively passed around a large bag of confetti so that everyone was holding a couple of fists full.

When Alison and David came through the door, they got pelted with a barrage of confetti and cheers. By the time David got into the car, he was covered from head to toe in tiny, multicolored dots. Alison lagged behind a minute to say good-bye to her parents.

And then she hugged each of the girls.

"I guess the marriage is up to me and David now," she told them, "but this wedding couldn't have happened without all of you." She stopped to wipe away a tear, then went on. "So thanks for being here. Now . . . I'd better get going before I collapse entirely into hopeless blubbering."

She got behind the wheel and started up the ancient engine, then turned and put her head out the window and shouted, "See you all at Shelley's wedding!"

She put the car in gear and sputtered off.

CHAPTER
TWENTY

Sunday morning, before Dana, Faith, and Shelley left, the old and new girls got together in 407 for an informal breakfast, a kind of potluck with each of them bringing one of her favorite goodies.

Faith came armed with her old favorite, pretzels and mustard.

Dana contributed bagels she'd bought frozen in town, then heated up in Alison's toaster oven.

Shelley brought Alison's spaghetti pot filled with a concoction she called Iowa Cooler. It was a combination of orange, grape, and apple juice, with a shot of chocolate syrup.

Jane contributed a can of paté and a box of white crackers, her favorite snack.

Andy gave up all the rest of her most recent shipment of chocolate chip cookies.

Toby heated up her three remaining cans of Texas-style chili, then topped it with sour cream and shredded longhorn cheese.

"Wow, Toby. I didn't know you were a gourmet cook!" Andy said.

"Well, actually, I was going to make beef Bourguignon," she said, putting on a Boston accent to impersonate Jane. But with her Texas drawl creeping out from underneath, the effect was enough to send everyone into gales of laughter.

"Well, we got Alison married and off to Niagara Falls," Dana mused, passing around her bagels and a container of cream cheese.

"Do you think she'll live happily ever after?" Shelley wondered aloud.

"Oh, I think so," Faith said, dipping the end of her pretzel into the mustard jar. "No one could've looked happier about their future together than David and Alison yesterday."

"I'm really glad we came back for this," Dana said, taking a mug of Iowa Cooler from Shelley. She looked down into the cup. "Boy, does this stuff look gruesome."

"I know," Shelley admitted, "but it tastes great. Really." Everyone looked at their mugs dubiously.

"Come on," Shelley urged. "I know. Let's make a toast. To Alison and David!"

No one could say no to this, and so they all held their mugs high and then gulped the Iowa Cooler. And then looked at each other. And then broke into a six-way smile.

"Not bad, Shel," Dana said. "Not bad at all."

"Let's have another toast!" Andy shouted. "To the girls of 407 . . . past, present, and future!"

"Here, here!" everyone said. Then Faith added, "Even if certain occupants have changed the room's true spirit by putting boring beds in place of the magical floor islands, and by painting over its superb black walls with something suspicious called 'Wedgwood Blue.'" But she said this with a smile that let Jane and Toby and Andy know she was only teasing.

"I've got another toast," Dana said. "To the inner circle. To the six of us who have lived within these hallowed four walls, and therefor deserve to know its deepest secret."

The others looked at her questioningly, and so she explained. "The Mystery of the Tea Bag," she said, pointing toward the ceiling above Toby's bed.

"Yeah, Toby," they all said, as she got an inkling of what was to come and sprung up off the floor and ran laughing down the hall with the others following, trying to catch her, out of breath from mixing up laughing and running. Out onto the front lawn of Baker House, where all six of them tumbled into a huge pile of leaves and laughter and friendship.

When Toby and Jane work as waitresses in Andy's family's restaurant over Christmas break, they learn to dish it out. But can they learn to take it? To find out, read The Girls of Canby Hall #20, FRIENDS TIMES THREE.

Read All About
The Girls of Canby Hall!

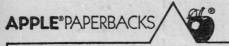